GAVIN'S SALVATION

RED LODGE BEARS - 3

KAYLA GABRIEL

GET A FREE BOOK!

Join my mailing list to be the first to know of new releases, free books, special prices and other author giveaways.

http://freeshifterromance.com

Gavin's Salvation: Copyright © 2019 by Kayla Gabriel

All Rights Reserved. No part of this book may be reproduced or transmitted in any form or by any means, electrical, digital or mechanical including but not limited to photocopying, recording, scanning or by any type of data storage and retrieval system without express, written permission from the author.

Published by Kayla Gabriel
Gabriel, Kayla
Gavin's Salvation

Cover design copyright 2019 by Kayla Gabriel, Author

Images/Photo Credit: Deposit Photos: svetas; cookelma; dashek

This book has been previously published.

ABOUT THE BOOK

Yeah, okay, so maybe sexy Gavin Beran has a little bit of a problem. He likes to pursue women who need "fixing", ride in on his white horse and save the day. He's well aware of his savior complex, as if his brothers would ever let him forget all the "broken dolls" he's helped in his life.

That doesn't stop him from being attracted to innocent, beautiful blonde Faith, a curvy werebear with more family troubles than the Jackson Five. One simple look at her leads to a kiss in the moonlight, which blows up in Gavin's face in three seconds flat.

Now Faith is on the run, clinging to her smoking hot savior and wondering how she's going to keep her V-card intact. Gavin's kindness only fans the flames of their desire, and soon passions spiral out of control.

This sensual, sweet BBW romance features intense chemistry, brawny men brawling, and a breathless chance at love... if only Faith and Gavin can reach out and grab it, hold onto it for dear life.

18+ for filthy language, naughty nights under the stars, and combustible adult situations!

1

Gavin Beran shifted in his seat, frowning at the cramped hardwood picnic table that he and two of his brothers had staked out as their territory. It was one of maybe two dozen or so that were scattered over a broad expanse of thick, green grass in the public park where the Krall clan had set up the third day of their week-long string of social activities, all geared toward getting single Berserkers together to find potential mate matches. It was like a singles' cruise, except with dozens of nosy werebear parents looking over their children's' shoulders the whole time. Also instead of sun and sea and fun, it was St. Louis and forced socialization and a lot of very brash females determined to find the strongest Alphas for their mates.

So... basically, it was hell. Gavin's parents, the Alpha couple of the Beran clan, had only managed to drag their sons to the event by promising to leave them alone for three full months afterward. Of course, half the men in the family were missing; Luke had vanished in pursuit of some long-lost Berserker female, and Noah and Finn had latched onto a couple of women on the first night of the St. Louis festivities. That left Gavin, Cam, and Wyatt in the sharks' tank, biding their time while proud mothers paraded their eligible daughters like prize-winning thoroughbreds on show.

Gavin looked at Cameron and Wyatt, both older than him by two and four years, respectively. Cameron was impeccably dressed, looking every bit the city slicker in his expensive dark jeans, dark blue plaid button-up shirt, and charcoal gray sweater with the sleeves rolled up to reveal matching sleeves of brightly-colored tattoos. Wyatt wore his usual jeans, snug white tee shirt, leather boots, and black leather jacket. Gavin looked down at his white Marvel Comics tee shirt, green cardigan, jeans, and Converse, feeling a little under-dressed beside his brothers. Still, with their dark hair, piercing turquoise eyes, and tall, thickly muscular frames, none of the Beran men were lacking for female attention, Gavin included.

Today's event was a huge all-day park picnic, complete with a veritable feast of fried fish and barbecue and games of horse shoes. They'd made it through the first three hours of awkward introductions somehow, and his parents had let the Beran brothers retreat to their own table, giving them a little distance from the crowd. Now Gavin, Wyatt, and Cam were just sipping beers, talking shit, and avoiding any potential love-struck ladies. In this setting, being tall, brawny, and good-looking was actually turning out to be a torment. For Gavin, at least. His brothers had certainly found their own diversions.

"Which one is Theresa?" Cameron asked, reaching

out and picking up a sheet of paper from several that Wyatt had laid out on the table.

"She's the really tall brunette that always talks about Pinterest," Wyatt drawled, a smirk on his face. His go-to expression, these days.

Cam grunted, giving his head a quick shake. He laid down the sheet of paper in favor of another, pursing his lips.

"If Stephanie is the redhead from Atlanta, you can't count her. I kissed her in the coat closet on the first night," Cam declared.

Wyatt's eyes sparkled, a grin spreading across his face.

"I did more than kiss her," Wyatt said. "A lot more."

"But I got to her first," Cam argued.

"I think level of activity outweighs the time stamp. And there was plenty of activity, if you get my drift," Wyatt said. He leaned on his elbow, quirking a brow as he sipped his beer.

"You two are hopeless," Gavin chipped in. "Seriously, this is both depressing and disgusting, all at once."

"You're just mad because you haven't gotten any action," Cam accused.

"I'm not involved in your idiotic bet," Gavin snapped.

"What the hell do you all think you're doing?" came a booming voice from directly behind Gavin.

Gavin tensed, knowing that his swaggering Alpha of a father was standing right behind him, no doubt looking down at the table where Wyatt and Cameron had laid out several sheets of names and tally marks, some stupid ongoing competition they had started over a month ago. Gavin glanced sideways, checking out his brothers' reactions to their father's question. Cameron's expression was carefully blank, while Wyatt bordered on bored insolence. Gavin turned a little in his seat so that he could see his father; he had nothing to say, really, but he had promised his mother that he'd keep the peace between Wyatt, Cam, and their father for the duration of their trip to Missouri.

"We're just keeping track of some things," Wyatt said to Josiah, his canines flashing as he gave a dangerous smile. Wyatt's big hand came out and swept up the papers, stacking them and turning them over in an easy motion.

"You three are supposed to be finding mates, not drinking and tossing skirts. And certainly not gambling," Josiah grumbled, shifting his accusatory glare between Cam and Wyatt before landing on Gavin. "And you... you're supposed to be watching them, not encouraging them."

"We're not kids," Cameron cut in. He was perfectly calm and collected, but Gavin knew that anger was simmering below the surface, ready to be unleashed at the slightest provocation. It had always been that way with Cameron, quick to anger and slow to remorse.

"We're older than him, anyway," Wyatt said, a calculating look on his face.

"I don't care. Gavin's the only one of you three that has any sense," their father declared. "If any of you do something to offend any of the other Alphas or their daughters, there will be a reckoning. Don't embarrass the clan."

With that warning and a deep scowl, he turned and

headed off to rejoin the party. There was a long moment of silence, stretching uncomfortably between Gavin, Wyatt, and Cam. When Wyatt flipped the papers back over with a smirk, Gavin rolled his eyes.

"What about Annabeth?" Wyatt asked Cameron. "Short, blonde, huge tits…"

Not waiting for Cam's reply, Gavin shoved to his feet with a long sigh. His brothers were badly behaved, and uncontrollable to boot. Gavin wasn't about to stand around and listen to their misogynistic crap for another second, especially not after their father's thinly veiled threats. No way in hell was Gavin going to play referee between his brothers and his father this time.

"Get us a beer, will you?" Cam called as Gavin stalked off. Gavin flipped them both the bird, garnering disapproving looks from a few older ladies as he went.

Gavin scanned the area, skirting most of the crowd as he sought a quiet spot. He'd just started reading a really good mystery novel on his phone's e-reader app, and it was calling his name. He just needed somewhere to be alone for a couple of hours. He spotted a cluster of trees, tucked away near the gravel parking lot. A little shade and privacy, just what he needed.

When he was twenty paces away, he slowed. He heard a woman speaking, her tone bright and lively.

"And the pony looked at the pile of apples, stacked wayyyy up to the sky…" The woman paused, her words drowned out by the sound of childish giggling. "And the pony at one apple, and another apple, and another… until he was so full he thought he would BURST!"

The laughter doubled, and Gavin imagined that the

woman must be pantomiming something silly. He moved closer, coming around just far enough to see the woman from the back. She sat on a plaid blanket, a dozen children spread out around her. From this vantage Gavin couldn't see her face, only that she was pleasantly curvy, with thick, straight, creamy blonde hair that flowed down past her shoulders. She wore a very conservative pale pink dress with long sleeves, her legs tucked up under her body so that only the white leather tips of her shoes peeked out from under the hem of the dress.

"And what do you think the pony did then?" she asked the kids, cocking her head.

"He puked!" a little boy shouted, excited. The woman laughed, shaking her head.

"No. He took a nap!" she declared. "What do you think it sounded like when he slept? Did he snore?"

The kids broke into raucous laughter, making loud snoring noises.

"Faith, Faith! What happened to the pony after his nap?" asked a little girl, reaching out to tug at the woman's sleeve.

"Well, Marissa, I can tell you for a fact that that pony lived forever on his island. That pile of apples grew and grew, so that he never ran out, and he spent every day playing on the beach and eating apples and napping in the sun," the woman confided.

The little girl gave a squeal of delight and flung herself on the woman, receiving a chuckle and a hug for her efforts.

"Faith! Can we go tell Mama about the pony who ate all the apples?" a little boy asked, climbing to his feet.

"Of course, Adam. I think I could use a little break to think up some more stories. Why don't you all go get something to drink?" she told them. The kids took off in a jubilant flock, spreading out to find their parents. The woman turned to watch them go, amusement and affection playing over her features.

When Gavin got a good look at her, he let out a whoosh of breath. She was absolutely stunning. Her face was a sweetly rounded heart shape, with a pert nose and full pink lips. She wore no makeup, but her finely arched dark brows and sparkling hazel eyes needed no emphasis. A smattering of delicate freckles covered the bridge of her nose and the apples of her cheeks, giving her an innocent, youthful look though she was probably in her mid-twenties.

When she noticed Gavin at last, she turned toward him with a bright smile that made Gavin feel like he'd been punched in the gut. Her smile dimmed after a moment, confusion taking over.

"Oh... hello," she said, her brow furrowing. It was everything Gavin could do to untwist his tongue enough to speak to her.

"Hey. Nice story," he said, giving himself a shake and moving toward her. She laughed, a beguiling pink flush rising in her cheeks.

"Thanks," she said with an unassuming shrug.

"Mind if I sit with you?" Gavin asked.

"Oh..." She paused, her gaze going to the crowd, looking for someone. "I guess not."

"Do you have a jealous mate or something? I don't want to cause trouble," Gavin said, turning to look back at the crowd, half-expecting some huge Alpha to come barreling out of the crowd, ready to rip Gavin to shreds.

"No! No," she said, shaking her head. "Sorry. Please sit down."

He took a seat, giving her plenty of space. Reaching out, he offered her a handshake, surprised when she hesitated and looked around again before accepting. Her hand was small and soft in his, making his bear wake and take notice.

"I'm Gavin," he said, giving her what he hoped was his most charming smile.

"Nice to meet you," she said, her tone polite but curious. "I'm Faith."

She seemed unable to hold eye contact, looking down at her lap and smoothing her dress over her legs.

"So..." he said, trying to find a suitable topic. "I guess if you're not mated, those probably aren't your kids?"

Faith flashed a timid smile and shook her head.

"Some of them are my brothers and sisters, some of them cousins," she said.

"Brothers and sisters?" Gavin asked, raising a brow.

"My father remarried," she said, pointing out a small group of Berserkers crowded around one of the picnic tables. "The redhead, there, that's Sheila."

The group was perhaps ten men and five women, most in their twenties and late teens. One silver-haired man stood a little apart, a frown etched on his features. Gavin figured him for the Alpha, Faith's father. Gavin eyed them, his curiosity growing when he saw that the females all wore long-sleeved, full-length dresses like the one Faith wore. The men were dressed in dark slacks and button-up shirts, conservative enough to be somewhat unfashionable.

"How many brothers and sisters do you have?" he asked, keeping his tone casual.

"Fourteen," Faith said with a shrug.

"Holy shit," Gavin said, his eyes widening. "I have five brothers, and people are always blown away by that. You must get some interesting commentary."

Faith gave him another tentative smile.

"Yeah," she admitted. "It's kind of embarrassing sometimes, to be honest."

"I didn't mean to pry. I'm nosy, it runs in my family," Gavin joked.

"It's no problem," Faith said, her head dipping low. She picked at a loose thread on the blanket, cheeks flaming. Gavin was startled that the same woman who'd been so animated a few minutes earlier should now be so painfully shy.

"So... why aren't you mingling with all the other Berserkers?" Gavin asked.

Faith glanced up at him, her hazel eyes flashing with some emotion Gavin didn't quite comprehend.

"My clan is here to find mates for my brothers," she said, her words measured.

"That seems kind of strange. No offense," Gavin told her.

Faith shrugged a single shoulder, her gaze drifting back down to her lap.

"I don't have much say in the matter," was her only reply.

Gavin wondered how to respond, but he was saved

the trouble. A huge blond Berserker male was crossing the grass in broad strides, a scowling glare on his face.

"Uh oh," Faith whispered under her breath.

"Is that one of your brothers?" Gavin asked.

"Yeah. Jared is kind of... strict."

Gavin shot Faith a glance, wondering at her words. She was a grown woman, and the man was her brother, not her father... Gavin shook his head, unable to piece together the full puzzle. Faith's brother reached them in the next heartbeat, walking right onto the blanket. The blond man purposefully blocked his sister from Gavin's view, not stopping until he was practically touching Gavin.

Gavin leaned back, giving the man a skeptical glance.

"Can I help you?" Gavin asked.

"Yeah, you can," Jared replied, his accent thick as molasses. "You can get away from my sister, for starters."

Gavin took a breath, stifling his immediate impulse to stand up and pummel the guy into the ground. Nobody talked to a Beran man that way. Besides, he hadn't even done anything wrong.

"I was under the impression that this is a social event," Gavin said, keeping his tone even and his face blank.

"Not for her, it isn't. We're only here to find females for the unmated men, not to find trouble for the females we already have," Faith's brother answered, crossing his arms and leaning over Gavin a little further.

"That seems kind of sexist, doesn't it?" Gavin asked.

"What it seems like is none of your damned business. I asked you once already, and now I'm telling you. Get out of here and leave my sister alone. I don't want to say it again," Jared said, his voice rising.

Gavin held his hands up, unwilling to start a fight over a simple conversation.

"Alright, alright," Gavin said. "You mind backing up a little, there?"

The other man shot him another nasty glare that said he did indeed mind, but he took a step back. Gavin stood up, brushing himself off.

"Faith... Nice to meet you, I guess," Gavin said with a shrug. "Enjoy the picnic."

Gavin turned and headed back toward the party. When he reached the picnic table where Cam and Wyatt still sprawled, gossiping, Gavin looked back at the blanket.

Jared was leaning over Faith, his expression dark as a thundercloud. Jared pointed a finger in Faith's face, and she cringed.

"What's going on over there?" Cam asked, his gaze narrowing.

"Not sure. I'm gonna find out, though," Gavin said.

"What do you know, we've been here a whole seventy-two hours and Gav's already found himself a damsel in distress," Wyatt cracked.

"Shut the fuck up," Gavin snapped, not bothering to look at Wyatt.

"He's right, though. That is kind of your thing," Cam said.

Gavin turned, pinning them both with a glare.

"I'm probably going to butt heads with that asshole

again," Gavin said, jerking his thumb backward to indicate Jared. "Are you two gonna back me, or what?"

"A good fight? Hell yeah," Wyatt said.

"I happen to like damsels in distress too," Cam added, giving Faith a long look.

"You two are miserable. How come I never get stuck with Luke or Finn?" Gavin asked with a sigh.

Chuckling, Cam and Wyatt went back to discussing women and the stupidity of the whole mating ritual. Gavin only half-listened, his eyes going back to Faith again and again. If Faith's brother had meant to make Gavin lose interest, he'd certainly gone about it the wrong way. Gavin sighed, knowing that nothing good was going to come of this situation.

2

"I can't believe we're *camping*. I should have gone with Finn and Noah," Cameron groused, pulling his suitcase and a sleeping bag from the back of Wyatt's rental SUV.

"We're sleeping in cabins. It's not even real camping," Gavin pointed out.

"God forbid," Wyatt said, rolling his eyes at Cameron. "I think you're just scared that I'm going to kick your ass at the games tomorrow."

Cameron chuckled and shook his head.

"Keep telling yourself that, brother," Cam said. "First off, Gavin is going to outrun both of us. He's fast as hell and he actually runs regularly. Second, you've never been a good wrestler. Brawling at bars does not an athlete make."

"It's all about brute Alpha strength," Wyatt informed him, a smirk on his lips. Cam tensed, ready to start a confrontation, but Gavin cut him off.

"Save it for tomorrow, idiots," Gavin demanded.

"We've only been here for five minutes, so let's just settle in and find some diversion. I hear there's going to be a big drive this afternoon to bring in game and fish, and then a fish fry and cookout."

Gavin slammed the car trunk, hoisting his suitcase and sleeping bag, and led the way toward the cabins. The Berserkers had rented out several square miles of campsites and forest for the weekend; the rental included a few dozen clusters of squat brown wooden cabins clustered around covered entertainment pavilions. The largest pavilion had been marked on the campsite map, denoted as the primary social and food preparation area for the trip's duration.

"Let's see..." Gavin murmured to himself, looking down at the sheet of paper that held their cabin assignment. "Three-oh-five... three-oh-six... three-oh-seven! This is ours."

Using the provided key, he swung open the door and stepped inside. Their cabin had two main rooms, one with a kitchenette and a couple of worn sofas, and the other with four very basic metal-framed twin beds.

Gavin, Cam, and Wyatt all groaned in unison when they spotted the beds.

"We are gonna sleep like shit," Wyatt summarized.

"Like I haven't already spent the last two weeks missing my California king at home," Cam agreed.

Gavin tossed his suitcase and sleeping bag on the bed furthest from the door, then stretched.

"At least we're out of the car," he said. "Do either of you know where Ma and Pa are staying?"

"Way on the other side of the camp. Most of the

Alpha couples are in a single site together, and the rest of the sites are broken up by clan or what part of the country you're from. No men and women in the same cabin, either," Cam said.

Wyatt and Gavin both looked at him, brows raised.

"What? Ma gave me the low down yesterday. Said she wanted us to keep out of trouble," Cam said.

Wyatt dumped his stuff on another of the beds and looked around the room, his distaste evident.

"There had better be some seriously hot women on this trip," Wyatt sighed.

"Only one way to find out, eh?" Cam suggested, nodding toward the cabin's front door. "In any event, I'm starving. Maybe we can catch a nice fat deer and wow all the ladies with our impressive hunting skills."

Gavin could only shake his head and follow his brothers, intent on keeping them in line.

3

Several hours, several deer, and countless ice chests of fish later, the festivities were in full swing. Gavin emerged from the cabin, freshly showered after putting in an hour of gutting and cleaning fish for the fish fry. He thanked his lucky stars he'd grown up at Red Lodge, with his father teaching him how to provide for himself; some of the men at the gathering were downright squeamish about butchering their catches, and the Beran men had been in stitches about it all afternoon.

As Gavin made his way toward the main pavilion, he saw dozens of Berserkers ambling and cavorting in their bear forms, wandering around the camp's dirt paths. The sight made his chest tight with pleasure, just seeing his people in their natural forms. A rare sight, but something that made him feel proud to be a bear shifter.

He thought of what might happen if a human stumbled into their midst. How panicked they would be, seeing bears of every shape and size, running and growling and tackling one another to the ground. The idea made him laugh out loud.

Gavin was so caught up in his thoughts, his eyes on his feet as he moved, that he didn't notice Faith until he slammed into her as she stepped out onto the path. His sheer size knocked her to her feet, scattering the contents of the wicker basket she clutched, fruits and vegetables rolling everywhere.

"Oh!" Faith huffed, eyes wide. She wore a simple gray cotton dress, covering her from neck to ankle. Her shiny blonde hair was braided and pinned up, an elegant touch.

"Ah. Sorry about that, Faith," Gavin said. "Wasn't watching where I was going."

"N-no problem," Faith replied, eyeing him nervously for a moment before looking around at the spilled produce.

"Here, let me give you a hand." Gavin reached out to help her up, unable to help but notice the way she blanched before she slid her hand into his. He saw her shiver at the contact even as she blushed, as if she were doing something altogether elicit.

"I... uh... I should have been looking, too," Faith babbled, ripping her hand from his the second she was on her feet. After brushing off her dress, she started picking up the potatoes and corn and plastic-wrapped pints of strawberries and blueberries. Gavin saw that she turned her body at a certain angle, making sure that she wasn't showing him her backside as she bent to retrieve the items. An oddly modest habit, to be certain.

"No problem," he said, helping her pick up the last

two pints of fruit. He handed them over as she tucked everything back in the basket and covered them with a checkered tablecloth.

Faith looked up at him, worrying her bottom lip with her teeth. Her gaze slid away to the dirt path from which she'd appeared, and a line of worry creased her brow.

Gavin frowned, his gaze traveling over to where she was looking.

"Is your brother coming or something?" he asked.

"No. Um. No," Faith said, changing the subject. "Are you going to the fish fry? I'm taking this stuff over there."

"Yep. Mind if I walk with you? I don't want to get you in trouble," Gavin said.

A flare of anger lit Faith's eyes for the barest second, and it gave Gavin hope. Perhaps Faith wasn't as meek as her brother would like, after all. He might control her, but it seemed that some small part of her would not be tamed.

"I'd like that," she said, to Gavin's surprise.

"Let me take that basket," he offered. She handed it over with a quick smile, her head dipping as they started off.

Gavin took the moment to admire the sleek line of her neck, the fine curves of her body under that bland dress. His lips twitched when he realized that no matter how Faith dressed, there was no hiding her femininity.

When they reached the main area, dinner was in full swing. There were tables piled high with freshly fried fish and venison, plus every side dish and dessert imaginable.

"This looks amazing," Gavin said.

"Yeah, I guess I was a little late bringing the basket," Faith said as she scoped out the feast.

"I don't think it will be missed," Gavin said with a wink. Faith blushed again, but dipped her head in silent agreement. "Why don't we get a plate and find a table together?"

Faith bit her lip again, looking torn.

"I'd like to, but... I'm worried that my brothers won't like it."

"What if we go sit with my parents? Surely no one can object with chaperones like that," Gavin suggested.

After a long beat, Faith nodded.

"That sounds good," she said.

"Cool. I'm definitely ready to try some of this venison," Gavin said, leading her to the buffet line. He piled a plate high with food, anticipating being able to burn it off later on a long moonlit run. He couldn't miss the fact that Faith hardly put anything on her plate; a piece of roasted fish, some salad without dressing, and a little fruit made her entire meal.

"That's it?" he asked, curious. Faith blushed like crazy, shifting back and forth on her feet.

"I'm not that hungry," she said. As she spoke, she looked off behind Gavin. When he turned, he saw her brother watching them both intently.

"Alright," he said, not wanting to increase her discomfort. "Hey, there's my Ma. Let me introduce you."

Without warning, Gavin grabbed Faith's free hand and tugged her toward the table where his mother and father sat with Gavin's Aunt Lindsay.

"Don't worry, they won't bite," Gavin told Faith.

Before she could answer, they were at the table. Gavin's family looked up, curious.

"Guys, this is Faith. Faith, this is my father Josiah, my mother Genny, and my Aunt Lindsay."

"Faith, nice to meet you!" Gavin's mother responded instantly. She stood and offered her hand, which Faith took.

"Are you from the Krall clan?" Gavin's father asked, taking Faith in with his sharp gaze.

"No. My father is Aros Messic," Faith said.

From the way his father's brows rose, Gavin could tell that there was a back story there, but he said nothing.

"Well, nice to meet you," Josiah said.

"Sit, sit!" Aunt Lindsay said, indicating the two empty seats at the end of the picnic table. Gavin took the one next to his father, leaving Faith the seat opposite, next to his mother.

"So, Faith, what do you do?" Gavin's mother asked.

"I'm a preschool teacher," Faith said, giving Genny a soft smile.

"Oh, how nice!" Genny beamed, glancing at Gavin. Gavin repressed a sigh; his mother was the eternal matchmaker.

"Gavin's a social worker," Aunt Lindsay told Faith.

Faith glanced at Gavin, interest lighting her expression.

"So you help people for a living, huh?" Faith asked.

"I try, at least," he replied with a shrug.

"Well, you both work with children," Genny pointed out.

Gavin nodded and dug into his food, savoring the fried fish and potato salad.

"Faith is quite the storyteller," Gavin told his family. "I met her yesterday because she was telling a very animated story about... what was it, a goat?"

Faith laughed.

"A pony, I think," she said. "My mother used to tell me stories about a pony who wanted to eat everything he saw, and it seems to be as popular as ever."

"Whereabouts are you from, Faith?" Genny asked.

"Centralia, across the river in Illinois," she answered. "Less than forty-five minutes from here."

"Do you have a big family?" Lindsay asked.

"Guys, let her eat. Jeez," Gavin interrupted.

"No, no, it's okay," Faith said, her eyes sparkling. "I have fourteen brothers and sisters."

"Good lord!" Josiah barked. "That's some kind of kin you've got there."

"It's never lonely," Faith agreed.

"Did you get some of this chocolate cake?" Lindsay asked, motioning to the piece on her plate. "It's German chocolate, incredible."

"Ah... ummm, I didn't," Faith said, her eyes dropping to her plate. She toyed with her fork, pushing around a few pieces of fruit but not actually eating anything.

"Not a chocolate lover?" Lindsay asked.

"We keep a strict diet in our family," Faith said, lifting a shoulder. Her gaze went up again, searching, and when Gavin looked up he saw that Faith's brother Jared was watching their table like a hawk. He looked deeply displeased, despite the fact that Faith could hardly be more well-chaperoned.

"Well, I had some of that roasted fish that you have, and it is delicious," Genny jumped in. "Perfectly done."

Faith smiled, a soft dimple flashing in her cheek. She took a bite of the fish and nodded in agreement.

"I'm just glad I'm being fed," Gavin said. "My secret is that I'm a good cook, but I'm lazy. I eat out a lot more than I'd like to admit."

"I love to cook. Baking, especially," Faith said. "I bake a lot of bread. I know that carbs are terrible for you, but I can't seem to help myself."

"Carbs, schmarbs," Genny said. "You should eat what makes you happy. I just make sure I go for a nice walk every afternoon, and that keeps me in fighting form."

Faith looked thoughtful.

"I don't get out of the house as much as I'd like," she admitted. "There's always something going on at home, some fire to put out. I'm the oldest girl, so I'm in high demand."

Everyone laughed.

"I can only imagine," Genny said.

"Faith, will you be watching the wrestling and races tomorrow? Maybe you can come watch with us," Lindsay suggested, giving Gavin a sly look. It appeared that his Aunt was just as much a match maker as his mother.

"I'd like to, but... I'll have to ask my father," Faith said, setting down her fork.

Gavin noticed the black look that came across his father's face, and made a note to ask him about it later.

"Maybe Pa could ask," Gavin offered, nodding toward his father.

"No! I mean... I don't think that's necessary," Faith said, looking a little stricken at the idea. "I'll talk to him."

"You really should. You can meet two of Gavin's brothers, Cameron and Wyatt. They're entertaining," Aunt Lindsay chuckled.

Gavin shot her a quick glare. A sweet, innocent blonde like Faith would be all too tempting to his mischievous brothers. There was no way in hell she was going to become part of their moronic bet.

Across the clearing, Gavin saw that Faith's brother was beckoning to her with an impatient gesture. Gavin scowled, trying to understand how the man could possibly hold so much sway over the whole family.

"I'd better go. See you tomorrow, maybe?" Faith asked Gavin.

"It's a date," he said. Faith blushed and laughed, that dimple flashing again. She said her goodbyes to his family and then went to her brother's side, soon after vanishing from the pavilion altogether.

"Alright. What's the deal?" Gavin said, turning to his father.

Josiah shifted in his seat as he watched Faith and a couple of her siblings leave the pavilion. He looked contemplative for a moment, then grimaced.

"Aros Messic is not a good Alpha," Josiah sighed. "What little I've seen of him, mostly through yearly meetings of the Alphas' Council, has not been pleasant. He's so straight laced that he makes me look like a liberal, and he's fanatical in his beliefs."

"I'm almost hesitant to ask what those beliefs are," Gavin sighed. "Faith seems pretty afraid of him. Her brother, too."

"One of Aros's sons is his right-hand man. Jamie, or Jim..." Josiah said.

"Jared, I think," Gavin supplied.

"Right, sure. Well, they keep the old ways. And by old, I mean they are still worshipping Odin and Freyr and Thor. I don't know all the details, but I know that Aros considers modernization to be evil, and rules his children and clan accordingly. He advocates for a return to the old ways, before industrialization."

Gavin sucked in a breath, his brow furrowing.

"You mean... He's not just anti-computer, he's anti-*train*?" Lindsay asked, mirroring Gavin's own thoughts almost exactly.

"His whole family lives off the grid. They farm and raise livestock, and only consume what they produce. Frankly, I'm surprised to see the clan here. I can't imagine that any of the women at this event would give up their whole life to live in rural Illinois, without so much as a telephone," Josiah said.

"Why anyone would want to do that, I don't know," Genny added. "And it's not like Aros has any great success to point to as evidence of his ways being the best. The whole clan is poorer than dirt. I heard a rumor that his first wife had to give birth in a field once."

His mother shuddered, tsking.

"Why don't any of them run away?" Gavin asked.

"It's like a cult, centered around the Berserker legacy. Aros uses our kind as an example, saying that the Norse gods are every bit as real as you and me. He and his kin have all reared their children up to believe every word he says, and those who disagree are kicked out of the clan."

Gavin understood that threat all too well. Less than two months ago, the Alphas' Council had leveled that very threat on any mating-aged Berserker who hadn't managed to take a mate within twelve months of the decree.

It meant losing any Berserker friends and family, yes. But it also meant being denied access to the many Berserker wilderness preserves and refuges, some of the only places where it was truly safe to run free in bear form. Berserkers with no clan affiliation might have to go as far as South America or British Columbia to find a big enough stretch of land to roam *au naturel* safely.

"Why hasn't the Alphas' Council done anything about him?" Gavin asked, perplexed.

Josiah shrugged, looking a little guilty.

"He's a pain in the ass, but he has the right to run his clan however he wants. Running him off from the Alphas' Council would only mean that we have even less idea what he's cooking up out there in the woods. At least now we can keep an eye on him."

"He's a nasty piece of work," Gavin's mother chipped in. "I'm surprised that Faith has such a level head, coming from that clan."

Gavin could feel his mother's curious gaze, no doubt trying to fit Gavin and Faith together like puzzle pieces.

"Do yourself a favor and steer clear of all the men in her family," his father said. "Every single one I've ever met has been spoiling for a fight, and they don't pull punches. She's a nice enough girl, but..."

"Great, okay," Gavin cut his father off. "I think I'm going to catch up with Wyatt and Cam."

Pushing up from the table, he snatched up his half-empty plate and headed off to find his brothers. In the back of his mind, though, he couldn't stop thinking about Faith's wide-eyed beauty.

4

Faith Messic lay on her sleeping bag in the darkened bedroom of the cabin she shared with her sisters Debra, Shannon, and Lacey. She stared up at the ceiling, repressing a restless sigh. When her brother Jared found her eating lunch with the Beran family, he'd towed her behind right back to the cabin. Then her father had started in. After dressing her down in front of the whole family, calling her a *light-skirt*, whatever that was, he'd commanded Faith's sisters to watch her closely. *Lest she lose the remainder of her morals*, he'd said.

Faith bit her lip, trying to stay still. She'd played nice all night, eating dinner at the clan's private pavilion and playing outdated board games with her nieces and nephews until bed time. Ignoring her sisters' whispered questions and curious gazes, she'd straightened her spine and put a smile on her lips, something she was used to doing.

In truth, Faith had grown very good at pretending to

be herself. Her old self, that was. The uneducated, unworldly version of herself that ceased to exist over three years ago, the one she brought back to life each day to please her father and brothers.

Closing her eyes, Faith wondered if she'd made the right decision when she'd convinced her father to let her attend community college and get her early education degree. It was an uphill battle, and once she'd talked her father into it she could hardly back down. Not even when her very first class had taken place in a computer lab, much to her dismay.

Faith pressed her lips together, holding back a giggle when she thought of her wide-eyed younger self. She'd been so sheltered that she'd required an extra semester of classes just to catch up on the history, math, and science principles she'd never learned in home schooling, and tutoring sessions in English composition, computers, and finance.

She'd never been truly happy since stepping foot on that campus, but of course it wasn't the education that was to blame. It was simply that there was no unlearning things learned, no unseeing the Internet or cell phones or soft serve ice cream. Before she'd started college, she could count the number of times she'd eaten in a restaurant on one hand.

But even at West Illinois Community College, a true hodgepodge of mis-matched souls, Faith hadn't fit in. She learned the delight of a fast-food hamburger at lunch, but then she went home to take her place in the kitchen with all the other women, kneading and baking bread for the whole clan. While her sisters and cousins laughed and joked together, Faith felt out of place, her head full of what felt like very *big* ideas.

When she'd applied for and got a job at the local preschool, working a handful of hours a week, she'd been pushed further out of sync with her family. Her brother Jared monitored her every movement, even going so far as to peruse every book she checked out of the library. He dropped her off and picked her up from work each day, without fail. Her father and brother were smothering her, oh so slowly, and they seemed to enjoy Faith's wilting smiles and stooped shoulders.

Faith rolled over onto her side, careful to be quiet. She pictured the way Jared had reacted when he'd found her sitting with Gavin the day before. When her brother told their father, the next two hours became a non-stop, hate-filled diatribe about how worthless, weak, and immoral the Beran clan members were. Her father had some very strong feelings about Josiah Beran and his sons, and it seemed that none of them were positive.

A new burst of listless energy filled Faith, and she couldn't stand it for another second. Sitting up, she slipped her feet out of her sleeping bag. She wore a long cotton night dress and thin cotton leggings, the standard pajamas that her father insisted on for all the unmated women in their family. Moving as silently as she could, she stood up and grabbed the rubber-soled house slippers and lightweight jacket that lay at the foot of her bed.

Faith held her breath as she snuck out of the cabin, her heart frozen with fear. Sneaking around after dark was no new activity for her; she often crept out the window of her second-story bedroom to sit on the roof and watch the stars. Slipping past her sleeping sisters and out of the house was a whole new level of disobedience, though. If she were caught, there would be hell to pay.

Once outside, she put on her slippers and went into the woods, cutting a broad arc through the trees that kept her far away from the cabins where the rest of her family slumbered. The moon was high and full as she emerged onto the main path that led to the rest of the camp site.

Faith paused at the place where several paths stood in the moonlight. From the right she could hear music and voices, signs of revelry happening at the main pavilion. Straight ahead were paths that led to individual clans' cabins. For a fleeting, crazy moment Faith wondered which might lead to Gavin, the most interesting occurrence in her life of late.

Shaking her head, she chose to turn directly left and head for the lake. The path went down and around in a wide circle, stopping at each of the many docks that dotted the lake shore. The first few docks she passed were in use, inhabited by happy couples, drinking and chatting and having fun.

Swallowing down her envy, Faith continued past several more empty docks until she found one that she felt was sufficiently far away from prying eyes. She walked down to the end of the dock, leaving her slippers behind, and sat down. After rolling her leggings up to her knees, she dangled her feet off the dock, letting her toes skim the chilly water.

Faith leaned back, letting her hair cascade down behind her. Closing her eyes, she smiled at the idea of moon-bathing. She hummed to herself under her breath, enjoying the stolen moment of freedom. Right here, in this moment, she didn't have to pretend anything or please anyone.

A rustle startled her from her thoughts. She turned her head, pulling her feet up. Two black bears, an enormous male and a smaller female, thundered down the path. She watched them pass the dock, glad for their complete disinterest in her doings.

Before she could return to her moon bathing, though, she saw another figure. Tall, dark-haired, and broad-chested, he wore a tight black t-shirt and black running shorts. He slowed as he saw her, the movement almost comical as he checked her out. For a heart-stopping moment, Faith almost took him for Gavin. But he was a bit older, and now that he moved closer she could see that he had a light beard.

The man turned and put his fingers to his lips, giving a long, ear-piercing whistle. Seconds later two nearly identical men came crashing through the trees. Faith's jaw dropped when she realized that one was, in fact, actually Gavin. He also wore running clothes, although his t-shirt and tight spandex pants were dark gray. An unladylike snort of laughter escaped Faith's lips, and she clapped her hand over her mouth.

Gavin motioned to what could only be his brothers, saying something to them in a low voice. They stared at her for a few seconds before turning and jogging off into the woods. Faith's stomach flip-flopped when she realized that he wasn't going to follow them.

"Hey, you," Gavin said as he approached, giving her a lopsided smile. He seemed uncertain, and Faith couldn't blame him. She'd been forced to play submissive and fearful both times they'd met, and he probably thought she was disinterested or even disdainful.

"Hey back at you," she said, tilting her head. She felt herself flush, and cursed inwardly. Everything she knew about flirting she'd learned from watching girls at her college. She felt clunky and silly, but... she really did want to flirt with Gavin.

"I'm surprised to see you out here so late," he said. Faith could tell that he left of the most surprising part, that she was *alone*.

"I snuck out," she admitted. "Hopefully you won't tell on me."

Gavin's brows raised, his beautiful aquamarine eyes lighting with humor.

"Is that so? Hmm. I wonder if that means I might come sit next to you without getting my ass kicked by your brother," he said, flashing her another grin.

Faith pretended to consider him, her eyes taking in the six-and-a-half-plus feet of him, every inch more perfectly shaped than the next. He was muscular without being beefy, naturally tanned, and altogether drop-dead, darkly handsome. And those eyes... it was clear that Gavin was intelligent, kind, and funny.

"I guess you can sit next to me," Faith said at last, scooting over on the edge of the dock. Her heart thrummed in her chest, her mouth grew dry. What in the hell was she even doing talking to Gavin, much less ogling his body? She felt half ashamed, half a hopeless wallflower.

Gavin chuckled and sat down next to her, folding up his long legs in a graceful movement.

"So you snuck out. I wouldn't have guessed you'd do something like that," he said, giving her a long look.

"I'm not always so well-behaved," she said, her lips twitching upward into a smile. "Not when my family's not around, anyway."

"Ah, so that's the trick. I guess this is a pretty lucky moment, then. Maybe I have the stars to thank," Gavin said, looking up at the bright night sky.

"They are more beautiful than usual tonight, aren't they?" Faith sighed.

Gavin murmured his agreement, and for a long while they both just watched the stars. A thousand tiny thoughts swirled through Faith's mind at break-neck pace, impulses and fears and shivering bits of excitement.

"Do you like living with your family?" Gavin asked after a minute.

Faith opened her mouth, then stopped the automatic, defensive words in their tracks. She considered his question, then shook her head as she looked over at him.

"No, not really. It's... lonely," she said.

"With all those people around?"

"Especially then," she rejoined. "I'm not the person my family thinks I am. Or maybe just the person they want me to be."

Gavin didn't respond immediately, seeming to digest her words. His next statement took her a little by surprise.

"If you could do anything, anything you can't do now, what would it be?" he asked.

Faith looked at him for a beat, then glanced out across the lake as she mulled over his question.

"Can I have two things instead of just one?" she wondered.

Gavin chuckled and nodded.

"Of course."

"Well, I'd write a children's book, with my own illustrations," she said.

"Would it be about a pony who ate everything he saw?" Gavin asked, looking amused.

"Definitely," Faith said without hesitation. "It's a great story, if I do say so myself."

"And the second thing?"

Faith was silent for several moments before she replied.

"I'd talk to my mother," she said.

"Your mother... she isn't..." Gavin seemed unsure how to phrase his thought.

"Dead? No, I don't think so. My father always says she's 'gone', but I think she's out in the world somewhere, living a new life," Faith said. She flushed, biting her lip. "I'm not sure why I told you that. It's probably more than you need to know."

"Not at all," Gavin disagreed. "It's honest. I like honesty."

"I wonder what you must think of us, my family," Faith said, looking up to meet his gaze dead-on. For the first time in a long time, she really wanted to know how someone else perceived her clan.

"I think it seems pretty restrictive," he said. "Your brother seems pretty overbearing."

"Only because you haven't met my father. He's much worse."

Gavin nodded, but didn't seem overly judgmental.

"Why don't you leave?" he asked.

"Where would I go?" Faith asked, giving a humorless laugh. "St. Louis is the farthest I've ever been from home, and I've ever been alone in my life. I don't own anything, and the only thing I'm qualified to do is teach toddlers. I wouldn't last a month on my own."

"What's the worst thing that happens? You try, maybe you fail. At least you tried," Gavin said, his brow hunching.

"They wouldn't take me back. If I ever left, it would be for good. I'd never see my sisters or nieces and nephews again," Faith told him flatly. "When I said alone, I meant it."

Gavin started to say something, then seemed to think better of it.

"Well, at least you're not alone right now," he offered.

Faith glanced at him, her humor returning.

"No, I guess I'm not."

The moment felt inevitable, unstoppable. Before she knew it, Faith was leaning closer to Gavin even as he slid closer to her. His hand brushed her waist, making her shiver as he reached up and pushed back the thick curtain of her blonde hair.

The instant that her eyes closed, his lips brushed hers. His mouth was soft yet warm, his scent earthy and male, and she could feel heat radiating from his skin. Faith leaned further, letting her shoulder and side lean into his hip, his waist, his firmly muscled chest.

Gavin's lips worked ever-so-gently against her own, parting them with a soft flick of his tongue. She wanted to moan, or sigh, or scream, but the tip of her tongue touched his and suddenly she was burning up with hunger. Every inch of her skin was heated, anguished, wanting—

"Faith, what the HECK?" came her sister Lacey's voice.

Faith yanked herself upright, blinking in dismay as she turned to see her sister storming down the path toward the dock.

"Uh oh," was all Faith got out. In a flash, she saw Debra following behind, Jared in tow. Her father and several more of her brothers appeared next. For a fleeting moment, she thought she saw both of Gavin's brothers, too, but only one of them stepped out of the woods, hot on her father's heels.

"Odin's breath," Faith mumbled. "Maybe we should just jump in the lake and swim for it."

Gavin arched a brow at her, then rose to his feet and offered her his hand. Helping her up, he put his hand on the small of her back and steered her down the dock to meet the forming puddle of her family, seeming unaware of the way his touch made her shiver.

"What do you think you're doing out here with my daughter?" Faith's father thundered as he bore down on them.

"Talking?" Gavin said, keeping his cool.

"Faith, get over here," Aros bellowed. Jared came to stand next to him, mirroring his fury perfectly. When

Faith didn't move, rooted to her spot, Jared reached out and grabbed her by the wrist and yanked her close.

"I knew it, you slut," Jared growled. "I knew you couldn't be trusted. Out here having some, some tryst—"

Jared blustered, releasing Faith's wrist only to grip her just where her shoulder met her neck, his favorite method of restraint. His fingers dug into her flesh, the pain a sharp burst that nearly took her to her knees.

"Don't you dare—" She heard Gavin say. Faith tried to shake her head, to tell him not to get in the middle of it, but her tongue wouldn't comply.

"Get back, you," her father grated, reaching out and pushing Gavin back a few feet. "You'll not touch my daughter again."

The darkness that filled Gavin's expression startled Faith, made her cringe.

"Get your hands off my brother, old man," came another voice. Gavin's brother stepped up behind Faith's father, looking murderous. Where Gavin looked outraged, his brother looked... almost eager, somehow.

"You Berans," her father spat. "Always putting your noses where they don't belong. This is a family matter. Jared, bring her."

Her father spun, ready to leave. Jared turned, taking Faith with him, and that's when she saw that a crowd had gathered at the end of the dock. Gavin's father was elbowing his way through the group, the other brother at his side. At the edge of the trees, Faith spotted Gavin's mother and aunt. Her humiliation was now complete and absolute.

"Wait," Gavin shouted as Jared pulled Faith toward

the crowd. "We're going to be mated! She's under my protection!"

Everyone stilled. Faith could feel the hot, furious gazes of her father and brother trained on her.

"Is this true?" her father asked, teeth clenched.

Faith opened her mouth, but Jared gave her a hard shake.

"You'd better say it's not," he hissed. "If you bring shame to our family, I will make you suffer. You can't run from me."

That statement, more than anything, catalyzed Faith to action.

"It's true," she cried. "Gavin asked me to be his mate. I said yes."

Jared roared as he forced her to her feet, madness glinting in his eyes.

"You're going to wish you were never born," he promised. His skin rippled, his bear ready to emerge. Then Gavin and his brother stepped between them. Gavin knelt, pulling Faith close. His brother gave Jared a cocky grin as he reached out and gave Jared a forceful push, knocking him clear off the dock and into the lake with a great *splash*.

"Fucking asshole," she heard Gavin's brother mutter.

"Gavin," she said, clinging to him. She peered up at him, her fingers digging into his forearms as she desperately tried to... thank him? Warn him?

"Shhh, it's okay," he said. In the next instant, Gavin wrapped her in his arms, protecting her and giving her suddenly-chilled body a much-needed blossom of warmth.

"Alright, break it up!"

Faith saw that Josiah Beran was trying to disperse the crowd.

"She's going to our camp site for the night," Gavin's father informed the crowd.

"Like hell!" Faith's father protested.

"In one of the womens' cabins," Josiah clarified. "With guards outside, in case anyone tries any funny business. After that little show, she's not going back with you."

Several people in the crowd nodded, seeming satisfied with the conclusion.

"I agree," said another silver-haired Alpha, crossing his arms and directing a glare at Faith's father. Behind them, Jared was clawing his way back onto the dock, dripping and sputtering.

Gavin rose and pulled Faith to her feet. When she wobbled, tears stinging her eyes, he simply scooped her up and carried her through the crowd. Shame burning her through and through, Faith turned and burrowed her face into his chest as she held in the sob that was desperately trying to escape her chest.

Gavin carried her all the way to one of his family's cabins, straight inside and to one of the beds. Faith sucked in a deep breath, smelling him everywhere as he deposited her on the sleeping bag.

"Wait, this is your bed!" she said, wincing at how girlish she sounded. She thought him handsome, of course, and they were fake-engaged now, but...

"My mother is going to come stay with you. I'll be outside with my brothers, keeping watch," Gavin said.

Faith went from shy to deflated in a second, flat.

"Oh," she said, her voice small.

"I don't want to cause any more scandal, that's all. Half the clans in the country are watching us right now," Gavin said, reaching out and brushing a strand of hair from Faith's eyes. "If I stayed in here with you, it would look… It would take away some of your choices."

"Okay," she sighed, feeling ridiculous.

"Knock knock," Genny Beran said, coming into the room.

"Hey, Ma," Gavin said. A look passed between mother and son, something tender that Faith didn't quite understand.

"Alright, get along with you," Genny said, shooing Gavin out. "I'm sure Faith is quite tired, aren't you dear?"

Faith gave her a thankful smile, nodding. To her surprise, she actually was more tired than she'd realized. Gavin gave her a quick wave.

"See you in the morning, ladies," he said as he disappeared.

Faith let out a long gust of breath, rubbing her face with her hands.

"Faith…" Genny said, her expression compassionate. "It's going to be okay."

Faith actually laughed, a garbled sound.

"Is it? It doesn't feel that way," she said. "Gavin and I aren't really—"

Genny cut her off with a gesture.

"No need for details, my dear. Of all my sons, Gavin has the biggest heart. I'm sure he's done whatever needed doing."

Faith glanced up at her.

"Thank you," she said. "Really, your whole family is too kind."

"Pssh," Genny said. "Now, is it alright with you if I turn off the light? I really am tuckered out after all the excitement."

"Of course," Faith said, lying back on Gavin's sleeping bag.

"Goodnight, dear," Genny told her, turning out the light and rolling over. After a handful of minutes, Faith could hear the woman's dozing snore.

Only then did Faith begin to relax, burying her nose in Gavin's bedding, inhaling his wonderful scent as she began to drift off to sleep.

5

Gavin looked up from his cup of coffee as Cameron and Wyatt plunked themselves down across from him on the picnic table. He'd been in this spot half the night, within sight of the front door his cabin, turning his new situation over and over in his mind.

And yet, with the morning light peeking over the treetops, he still had no clear solution. He couldn't leave Faith with her crazy, abusive family. Wouldn't leave her, if things came down to it. On the other hand, if she resisted, could he force her to come with him? If he did, would he be any better than her father or brother?

"Ach, he's got the face," Cam said, elbowing Wyatt.

"He does," Wyatt agreed. "Mated face. Note the misery."

"Fuck off," Gavin sighed, leaning his elbows on the table as he glared at his brothers.

"After our help last night," Cam chuffed. "The thanks we get."

"You two are starting to sound like the twins, talking back and forth to each other," Gavin told them.

Wyatt looked at Cam, and they both shrugged in perfect unison. Then they cracked up laughing.

"Jesus," Gavin muttered.

"Look, though. Seriously," Cam said, his laughter easing. "We know you're regretting not joining our little bet. Since you've bagged yourself a mate, probably a virgin too, we can tell you some stories to keep you warm at night."

"Out of brotherly love, of course," Wyatt added.

"A virgin?" Gavin said, rubbing his face. "God, you're probably right."

"That's a new one for you, bub," Cameron said. "Usually the girls you date have a list of exes a mile long. It's how they get all their emotional baggage."

Cam sat back with a satisfied smile, knowing he was grinding Gavin's gears.

"This doll's broken in a whole different way. Intriguing, I admit," Wyatt said, mirroring Cameron's pose.

"Did I already say fuck off? Because really, fuck off," Gavin told them.

"A guy's gotta have projects," Cam said to Wyatt. "Apparently Gav doesn't get enough sad sacks at work, beating their kids."

"I'd figure that keeping the peace at Red Lodge would fill whatever hole is in his heart, but apparently not," Wyatt replied.

Gavin started to tell them to fuck off again, then stopped. He narrowed his gaze at his brothers, considering.

"Are you two... actually showing some kind of concern, albeit in the fucking rudest way you can? Is it possible?" Gavin asked.

Cam and Wyatt went quiet, looking at each other. Wyatt shrugged after a second.

"Look, if you want to tie yourself down to some virgin with a murderous family that's up to God knows what, that's your choice," Wyatt said. He avoided all eye contact, which Gavin took to mean that Wyatt was dead serious.

The cabin door opened. Faith emerged, followed by both Gavin's parents. Faith looked up and flashed him a troubled smile before dropping her gaze to her feet.

"The Messics are coming," Josiah grumbled.

Faith stopped in her tracks, looking like she was about to bolt.

"Faith," Gavin called to her. "Why don't you come sit by me, okay?"

After a long beat, she gave him another wobbly smile and did just that. She glanced over at Wyatt and Cameron. It was clear that she wanted to say something, but felt as though it was too private to say in front of his brothers. Gavin leaned close and whispered to her.

"We don't have to decide anything right now except whether you're going home with your family. Okay?" he asked.

Faith looked at him, her hazel eyes bright with emotion. She gave him a tight nod, biting her lip.

"Do you want to go home with them, or come with us?" Gavin asked.

Faith glanced away, sucking in a deep breath. When she looked back, she seemed decided.

"I can't go home," she whispered back.

"Okay. That's all you need to say. Just let us do the talking, and we'll be out of here in no time."

Gavin reached out and took Faith's hand, tucking her fingers in his own. Her brow furrowed, and for a second it looked as though she might cry. Instead she shook her head, giving his fingers a soft squeeze.

Gavin's chest tightened at the gesture, something uncoiling within him, fierce and protective and hungry.

Faith's father stepped into the clearing, her brothers tight on his heels. He made to walk right up to Faith; Gavin came to his feet, not releasing Faith's hand. His brothers stood behind him, but ultimately his father stopped the other Alpha's progression with a simple gesture.

"That's far enough," Josiah said. "Let's keep things peaceable."

"Bringing my daughter here without my permission doesn't exactly seem like a peaceful gesture," Aros said, planting his feet wide and crossing his arms.

"She's my son's future mate now. Do I need to get out the Alphas' rule book, Aros?" Josiah challenged.

"I think this is all for show, though I don't understand the reason," Aros said. He turned to Faith, giving her a hard look. "You can still come back with us now if your virtue is intact, Faith."

Faith's face went completely red, tears welling in her eyes. Gavin felt rather than heard the low growl that escaped his chest. He tugged at her hand, pulling her closer. That she let him slip an arm around her waist soothed him and his bear in a deeply primal way.

"I'm not... I'm not coming back," Faith managed, her voice just above a whisper.

"You'll be banished from the clan. You understand that, right?" jeered her brother, taking a big step forward.

"Don't make me make you back up," Wyatt growled, taking several strides toward Jared.

"Stop," Josiah said, holding up a hand. Wyatt stilled, but he did flash his canines at Faith's brother. If the situation were less serious, Gavin might have laughed at his brother's antics. Of course, he actually knew Wyatt. To a stranger, Wyatt was nothing short of a promise of violence.

"If you insist on taking her, then so be it," said Aros. "She'll be nothing but a burden, as she has been for us."

"No one fights for a burden," came a feminine voice.

Every eye turned to Gavin's mother, standing tall and proud near the cabin.

"You allow your mate to speak for you now, Beran?" Aros asked with a cruel laugh.

"She's wiser than anyone I know. I'm proud to have her speak for me," Josiah said. He bristled, clearly trying to keep his bear in check. His mate was Josiah's one true soft spot, a topic sure to get him in a no-holds-barred fight in seconds.

Aros spat on the ground, his face screwed up with disgust.

"You're weak," he said.

"Get Ma," Cam said to Gavin. "Take her and Faith to the car. We'll meet you there."

Aros and Josiah were arguing now, but Gavin wasn't listening to them anymore.

"Like hell. I'm not leaving," Gavin said, scowling at his brother. "I want a piece of big brother over there."

"They're gonna snatch your girl. Maybe hurt Ma, too. Wouldn't put it past them. Would you?"

"Fuck," Gavin muttered, glancing at Faith. She looked scared out of her mind, and he could actually feel her fingers shaking as she clung to his hand. His mother on the other hand... when he look over at her, she was actually rolling up her shirtsleeves. As if her sons were about to let her bare-knuckle scrap with a bunch of burly Berserkers.

"Wyatt, keys!" Cam snapped. Without looking, Wyatt fished the keys to his rental car out of his pocket and threw them to Cameron, who passed them to Gavin.

"Fucking fuck," Gavin said, pulling Faith along behind him. He made a beeline for his mother, letting his brothers play defense as he half-dragged both women toward the parking lot.

They reached the car in less than a minute. Gavin unlocked the car and put both women in the back seat, giving them his most serious expression.

"If either of you unlocks this car, you're responsible for what happens to the other person. Do you understand? If you get out and someone hurts one of you, it's the unlocker's fault. Don't provide access."

Faith looked at him with big eyes, her throat working as she nodded. Gavin's mother crossed her arms and huffed as she sat back, looking displeased. Gavin closed the door and armed the alarm with the key fob.

He turned and hustled back toward the clearing, but his brothers and father met him halfway.

"What, it's over already?" Gavin asked.

"Some of the other Alphas showed up and cleared everybody out," Wyatt lamented.

"Shit," Gavin said, shaking his head.

"I know. Don't worry, I punched the hell out of that brother. Think I broke his nose," Cam said, looking cheerful despite the blood trickling from one corner of his mouth.

"I really wanted to be the one to break his nose," Gavin sighed.

"Next time, son," Josiah said, clapping Gavin on the back as they walked back to the parking lot.

"What now?" Gavin asked.

"Cam and Wyatt and I are going to go clean out our cabins, and then we're heading for the airport. I'm in need of some fresh air. Montana air, that is," Josiah announced.

Gavin couldn't help but think that he'd never heard such a good idea in his whole life.

6

Faith sipped her airport coffee, staring around at the busy terminal. Gavin and his parents had gone to sort out some administrative matters, namely getting Faith on a plane with no identification of any sort. She'd left the camp with nothing more than the clothes on her back, and it wasn't as if she carried around a license or passport. No need, when the women in her family were forbidden from driving anyway.

That left her sitting in Lambert International Airport's small concessions area with Cameron and Wyatt. Though the Beran family were basically all strangers to her, she'd barely exchanged a handful of words with either of Gavin's brothers. They didn't seem too inclined to change that, either.

As soon as Gavin and his parents went to deal with her identification issues, Cameron jumped up and headed for the gift shop. Faith could still see him across the terminal, browsing through the magazines.

"So. What's your deal?"

Faith turned to stare at Wyatt, who stood up and dropped into the seat beside hers.

"I— What do you mean?" she asked, blushing. There was something about Wyatt that put her off, made her feel deeply uncomfortable. He was one of the most good-looking men she'd ever met, but it was more than that. There was some edge to him, some darkness that made her want to flee.

"I'm just wondering how this all came to be," he said conversationally, crossing his legs and leaning back in his seat. "One minute, we're on a camping trip. The next minute, my brother is rescuing you like a princess from a castle. What's the deal with that?"

"I— I don't know what you mean," Faith said, squirming in her seat.

"Uh huh. So is it like, you two are fucking, or is it like he wants to fuck you and you won't let him yet, or what?" Wyatt asked, pulling a toothpick from his pocket and slipping it between his teeth.

"That is a horrible thing to say," Faith said, crossing her arms.

"So, not fucking yet. Got it. Can't say I'm that surprised. You look like a prude," Wyatt told her, his gaze raking up and down her body, seeming to find her lacking.

"Well, you're never going to find out," Faith snapped, tugging at her careworn dress and straightening her spine.

Wyatt threw his head back, chuckling.

"Nice. At least you got some spice. Most of the girls Gavin rescues are so *boring*.

"Maybe you should be looking through the gift shop with your brother," Faith said, turning her face away.

"He does that, you know. Gavin likes the broken little dolls, women he fix."

"That's really none of my business."

"Yeah, right. I'm looking at you, lady. You seem nice, I'm sure. But look at you, and your family, and then look at my family. We are not on the same page. Not even in the same book. There's only one reason a girl like you gets hooked up with a guy like my brother."

Faith turned to look at him again, her eyes widening in disbelief.

"Money," Wyatt mouthed, then smirked.

"You are... ugh," Faith spluttered.

"Well, what else would it be? If you wanted an Alpha male, you would have picked me or Cam. Gavin's the softy in the family, a good shoulder to cry on."

Faith's jaw tightened, and she dropped her gaze before she could say something she'd surely regret. Wyatt might be a jerk, but his family was indeed rescuing her. She didn't want to take the chance that she might alienate them all, not after they'd been so kind. Her brother Jared had her father's ear in all matters, perhaps it was the same with Wyatt and Josiah Beran.

"I gotcha. Stay silent. Just know that you won't get a dime for taking him as a mate. I'll make sure my brother is protected. And you'd better not trample on his feelings, either. You will regret it to your dying day," Wyatt promised.

Before Faith could respond, Wyatt stood up and strolled over to the gift shop, grabbing a few bags of candy. Faith held in the angry tears that threatened to break free, suddenly realizing that even this miraculous rescue from her brother and father wouldn't be without strife.

Perhaps there really was no happy ending in sight for her, Faith mused.

7

Faith couldn't keep herself from pressing her nose against the car window as Gavin drove them from the Lodge to the guest house. She was in complete awe of the view, all soaring white-peaked mountains and velvety green hills. Every inch of the landscape was painted with vibrant, stunning colors and exciting textures. From drab, boring Illinois to this...

"Almost there," Gavin told her, making her start. She turned from the window, flushing a little when she saw the humor in his expression.

"I must seem like a country mouse," she sighed. "It's just... I can't believe you get to live out here! It's so beautiful, I can't get enough of it."

"Well, I actually live in Billings. I'm usually only here on weekends," Gavin informed her. "I'm going to take an extended leave of absence until this is all settled, though."

Faith frowned, her spirits dipping.

"I don't want to keep you from working," she said.

"And how will we know when things are settled, anyway?"

Gavin eyed her, considering her words.

"I think we'll decide together," he said. "And I've accrued three months of vacation over seven years' time. I think I earned it, don't you?"

Faith pressed her lips together, unwilling to argue with him. Later, after she'd come up with a solid plan, they could renegotiate things. She looked out the window again, gasping when a dark building came into view.

"That's your *guest* house?" she cried. It was the same rustic-looking style as the Lodge itself, almost like an over-sized log cabin. This structure was smaller than the main house, but not by much.

"Yep. Ma likes to encourage visitors," Gavin said with a shrug.

His attitude was so casual as to be cavalier, and it occurred to Faith that he had no idea how lucky he was. She'd never describe Gavin as having a privileged attitude, but he didn't seem aware of how much his family had to their name. Faith's family hardly had two sticks to rub together, a source of constant contention and frustration.

Gavin pulled up in front of the house and hopped out, coming around to open Faith's door. He opened the trunk and pulled out his suitcase, plus a cardboard box of things that Genny had packed for Faith. Against Faith's protests, Gavin's mother had insisted on a stop at Target as soon as they were off the plane. Genny had piled an entire cart full of clothes and toiletries, refusing to hear a single word about it.

It had been the first time in her life that Faith had been faced with selecting and trying on pre-made clothes; most of hers were hand-me-downs or dresses she'd made herself from old patterns. Genny had instantly seen how shell-shocked Faith was, and had picked out tons of things for her to try on. Faith had outright rejected a few things as being way too immodest, but in the end Genny had just picked everything that she thought looked good on Faith.

Shaking her head at the memory, Faith stared up at the guest house.

"It's so nice of your parents to let us stay here," she said to Gavin.

Gavin snorted.

"Are you kidding? My mother would move you into the main house and care for you like a china doll if you let her. She thinks you're the best thing since sliced bread," he told her.

Faith gave him a suspicious look.

"I mean it!" Gavin said. "She's probably already online, ordering you more stuff. Prepare to be spoiled."

Faith looked down at the box, her stomach churning.

"This is too much," she sighed. "Can you stop her from ordering anything else?"

Gavin gave a snort and moved toward the house, clearly not even considering the idea. He opened the door and then moved back, bowing as he ushered her inside.

"My lady," he joked, giving Faith a wink.

She couldn't help but return his smile. Stepping inside, she marveled at the place's beauty. The front room was one large space, soaring windows and dark wood framing the kitchen and living areas.

"Bedrooms are back that way," Gavin said, pointing to a hallway to the far right. "There are three bedrooms, and each one has its' own bathroom. Take your pick, but you might like the one all the way to the left."

"This house is amazing," Faith said, feeling small for once in her life.

"Well, go ahead and explore. I need to run back to the main house to get the groceries and add some stuff to Ma's list."

He was out the door before Faith could utter a word.

"Men," she sighed to herself. Then she laughed, because she really didn't know all that much about men, outside her family. And if Gavin was this different than her father and brothers, chances were that Faith's experience didn't cover much at all.

Faith swallowed, trying not to think about the fact that this was the first night she'd ever spend the night in a strange house with a man who wasn't a blood relative. The very thought made her mouth dry, so she cleared her throat and propelled herself toward the bedrooms.

She went into the hallway and opened the first bedroom door, smiling when she saw it. It was very masculine, all dark wood and navy blue hues. There was another picture window in this room, although a cluster of trees partially blocked one side of it. The pine trees seemed to fit well with the room, somehow.

Moving down the hallway, she opened the second bedroom door. This room was very simple, with a small day bed on one side and a large oak desk on the other. It was done in cheerful yellows and blues, the furniture set to frame a large bay window with a padded seat. It was very warm and comfortable, inviting one to sit down with a cup of tea and stare out at the glorious Montana scenery. When she stepped out into the hallway, Faith was almost hesitant to leave the room behind.

At last she came to the third bedroom. Faith's jaw dropped. It was absolutely stunning. One whole corner of the room was glass, revealing an unparalleled view of the mountains. The rest of the room was perfect, pristine white everywhere she looked. An enormous dark wrought-iron bed was against one wall, towering with thick comforters and feather pillows.

"Oh my," she whispered, stepping inside. She sat her box on the floor by the bed, admiring the gleaming white metal desk and side table. There were two doors side-by-side, calling her name. She opened one to find an empty walk-in closet. The other revealed a gorgeous white bathroom complete with an over-sized claw-foot tub and a glassed-in, fancy-looking shower.

Backing out of the bathroom, Faith felt completely overwhelmed. She was freakishly, obsessively neat and clean, but she'd never slept anywhere that felt so... complete. There wasn't a single thing in this house that needed doing, and it just made her feel so confused. Everything in her life was a mess, and there was no way that she should be feeling *good* about the outcome of the St. Louis trip. Then again, she couldn't control much of what had happened so far. So was she really being bad? Tears formed in her eyes as she tried to grapple with the ridiculous moral aspects of her situation.

Faith flung herself onto the bed, refusing to let herself cry over something so stupid as feeling relaxed for once. Her body trembled for a few moments before she became conscious of the sensation of sinking into the bed, gravity pulling her down and down and...

When Gavin spoke, Faith jerked awake. He was perched on the bed next to her, his knee pressed against her hip.

"Was I right about the room?" he asked.

Faith blinked and shook herself awake. Flushing, she wiped at her mouth, hoping she hadn't drooled everywhere while Gavin was watching.

"Uh... yes," she said, remembering his question. "I love this room so much. It's so perfect."

"I noticed that you seem to like to tidy things," he said with a shrug.

"What? When?" Faith asked.

"You tidied everything in sight from the second we got in the car in St. Louis until we got to the Lodge. The back seat of my car has never been so thoroughly dusted with fast food napkins before. Also you rearranged everything in the airport lounge."

"I did not!" Faith protested.

"Don't worry, it's kind of cute," Gavin teased. Faith blushed a deeper red, if that was even possible.

"It's a nervous habit," she grumbled.

"You can nervous-clean my condo anytime, standing offer," Gavin joked.

Faith gave him a suspicious look.

"You're in a really good mood," she accused.

Gavin just laughed and patted her knee.

"Get up. I made dinner," he said. He sauntered out of the room, leaving Faith to freshen up and follow him to the main room.

When Faith emerged from her bedroom a few minutes later, she was greeted with the most incredible scent of roasted meat. Her stomach rumbled instantly, and she flushed all the way to the roots of her hair. She loved food as much as anyone, but being a slightly larger lady, she was always very conservative in what she ate.

"There you are," Gavin said, turning from the stove with a twinkle in his eye. He was barefoot, wearing dark, low-slung jeans and a snug navy blue t-shirt. He looked freshly showered after their flight, though he hadn't shaved. The stubble somehow only enhanced his all-American good looks, making Faith acutely aware that she was probably still disheveled from traveling and napping.

"It smells great in here," Faith said, trying to see what he was cooking as she moved into the kitchen.

"Have a seat," Gavin said, using a metal spatula to point out a seat at the kitchen's granite-topped bar. "I'm almost done. Just hang out for a couple of minutes and we'll be good to go."

Faith complied, perching on one of the bar stools.

"So what did you make?" she asked. "I can tell by scent alone that it's going to be incredible."

"I hope you like venison," Gavin said, flashing her a bright smile. "I did venison steaks, roasted cloves of garlic, pan-fried asparagus, and butternut squash."

Faith's jaw dropped.

"I thought you were a lazy cook?" she managed, perplexed.

"I am, believe me. Don't get used to this kind of pampering," Gavin teased, turning to stir the contents of an asparagus-laden cast-iron skillet. "I just thought it would be nice to have a fancy dinner for our first night here. Kind of... a date."

He half-mumbled the last, focused on his work. Faith was glad he wasn't paying attention to her at that moment, because she was sure her blush and look of total shock weren't very flattering. She cleared her throat, unsure how to respond to the word *date*.

Gavin had done her an enormous favor, sure. He'd helped her get away from her father and brothers, after they'd been caught lip-locked. He was only being chivalrous... right?

"Okay, I think we're ready to go," Gavin said, unaware of Faith's inner turmoil. "What do you want to drink? I've got a really nice bottle of red zinfandel, if that works."

Faith hesitated. She figured he meant wine, but she knew next to nothing about it. No one in her family drank alcohol, and she'd never had so much as a sip of wine in her life. She didn't want to be rude, though, so she just nodded her head.

"Cool. Let's move over to the table, then," Gavin said, scooping up two platters of food. "Grab the wine and the bottle opener for me?"

Faith jumped up and hurried after him, picking up the wine bottle and wacky-looking gadget from the kitchen counter. Gavin had already set the table with plates and wine glasses and even two silver candlesticks complete with slim white tapers.

"This is too much," Faith said, shaking her head at Gavin.

"No such thing," Gavin disagreed. "Wait, wait, let's do this right."

He settled the two platters on the table and took the wine bottle and opener from Faith's hands, putting them to the side. With a smirk and a tiny bow, he pulled out her chair.

"Oh...kay," Faith said, growing unbearably awkward. "Thank you, Gavin."

"No problem. No one can say I don't know how to behave on a first date, at least," he said, his voice full of humor. Faith's stomach churned, because the same certainly could not be said about her.

She'd never been on anything remotely close to a date. In her clan, there were a lot more women than men, so a lot of women were destined for spinsterhood. The women who did find matches were mated off to none-too-distant relatives by the Alpha's command; there was no dating or courtship involved.

"This looks amazing," Faith said, dragging herself out of her thoughts. "I just realized how hungry I am."

Too late, she cringed a little inwardly when she realized that her first comment had been about her appetite. If her father and brothers had taught her anything, it was that her size was not her best feature, and that talking about food only encouraged unkind comments.

"Well, yeah," Gavin said, nodding. "We haven't eaten a

real meal since the fish fry. And I don't remember you eating well there, either."

Mortification filled Faith's chest when she realized that Gavin had been paying attention to what she ate. Not a good sign. She'd have to be careful at meals here, just as she'd been around her father or Jared.

"You okay?" Gavin asked. Faith straightened her spine and gave him a smile. He really was incredible, and she should stop brooding like a teenage girl.

"Of course," she said, reaching for the platter. "Can I serve you?"

Gavin raised a brow, but gave her a slight nod. Faith gave him the lion's share of everything, serving him first, and then taking only small portions for herself. The venison steaks were huge, and while she gave Gavin a whole steak, she cut the second so as to only serve herself a third of the massive portion.

"I thought you were hungry!" Gavin said, giving her an odd look as he watched her set up her plate. Faith gave him a sidelong glance, adding a little more asparagus and butternut squash to her plate.

"My eyes are usually bigger than my stomach," Faith said, settling the platter back on the table. She didn't miss Gavin's skeptical gaze, but he was too polite to say anything more.

"Alright. Let's do the final touches," he said. He stood up and used a pack of matches to light the candles, then deftly uncorked the wine. He poured them both half a glass of wine, then sat down and picked up his glass.

"I feel like we should toast. What should we toast to?" he asked.

Faith thought for a second before responding.

"To new beginnings? Is that cliché?" she asked.

Gavin chuckled, but shook his head.

"Maybe a little, but it's apt," he said. "All right, then. To new beginnings."

They clinked their glasses together, smiles spreading over their faces. Faith lifted the glass to her lips and took a sip, repressing a wince at the liquid's bitter taste. They ate and talked, the conversation growing easier as the meal passed.

Gavin told Faith about his job working with Children's' Social Services, about the challenges and rewards he found in his work. Faith listened, finding herself a little envious of how much he clearly enjoyed his career.

"I have to contact the school I worked for, let them know I won't be returning," Faith said a few moments later.

"I think Cameron has an iPhone and a laptop coming for you in the next couple of days. That should make things easier. You certainly don't need a job here, but if you wanted to, you could start looking for a new position. If you found something in Billings, we'd work in the same area."

Faith looked at Gavin, trying to ascertain his meaning. He was making it sound as if they were already halfway to being mated, as though things were clear and open when in reality they were very much not so.

"Or what about your book?" he asked, continuing his thought.

"My book," she repeated, trying to mask her bafflement.

"Sure. If you wanted to work on your children's' book, that might be a good place to start. It's good to have a job you love."

Faith took a big gulp of her wine to cover her growing confusion. Gavin rose and gathered the dishes, refusing her help, and proceeded to clean up the kitchen, humming contentedly all the while.

"How about a movie?" he asked when he'd finished.

"That sounds nice," Faith said. It would give them something else to focus on, and give Faith time to think about what her next move might be. She couldn't just stay and live off Gavin's charity forever, after all.

Gavin gave her the choice of movie, pointing her toward half a wall of DVDs in the living room. Many of the films were titles she'd never heard of, popular dramas and comedies whose subject matter Faith deemed too risque for her first real evening in Gavin's company.

Eventually she settled on *Wall-E*, a family film about a cute, lonely-looking robot. It was way outside Faith's wheelhouse, but it seemed innocuous enough. The movie was visually breathtaking but had very little dialogue, and Gavin surprised her by chatting and sipping wine through most of it.

To her surprise, the movie ended up being wonderful. Gavin kept pouring a little more wine in her glass every half an hour or so. Curled up on the couch next to Gavin, Faith was soon pleasantly awash in relaxed, happy comfort.

Gavin pulled a soft white comforter off the back of the couch and spread it over them both, and Faith soon grew drowsy. Abandoning her wine glass, she let herself sink into the couch, leaning closer and closer to Gavin until she was pressed up against the firm warmth of his side. Eventually he stretched out and slid an arm around her shoulders, quieting as the movie's plot grew more intense.

Faith peered up at Gavin through her lashes, blushing madly as she realized how truly handsome he was, and how nice his body felt pressed against hers. The wine whispered to her softly, making her wonder if perhaps Gavin might kiss her again, wondering what she could to do make him press his lips to hers once more.

She never managed to find out, though, because her traitorous eyelids began to droop. She soon drifted off to sleep, enjoying the warm, safe nest Gavin had created.

8

Gavin came to a halt in front of the guest house, his lumbering bear form making his movements a little less than graceful. He watched Faith's bear as she turned to eye him with a snort, apparently not missing his fumble. He could see the laughter in her eyes, but it made him happier than he could express in his current shape.

Over the last ten days, Faith had truly begun to blossom. She was every bit as sweet and eager to please as he'd originally anticipated, but she was also witty, and interesting, and engaging. Once she'd relaxed and stopped fighting the pampering and lavish gifts from his family, Gavin found that she was equal parts charming and challenging, and wholly beautiful.

He'd never lived with any of his girlfriends, none of them had ever been that serious. So it was a pleasant surprise to find that finding Faith early in the morning, cooking pancakes in her overly modest pajamas and bathrobe and slippers, was altogether endearing. Though they mostly spent their days ambling in their bear forms, cavorting and fishing and exploring the Lodge's lands, outside breakfast time Faith always kept herself dressed very neatly and conservatively.

Gavin's heart had gone out to her when he'd come up behind her as she sat on the couch. He'd glimpsed the screen of her laptop, finding that she was researching 'How To Put An Outfit Together'. He supposed that this was a pretty big change for her, being in a strange place, bereft of her family, and expected to talk, act, and dress in ways that were unfamiliar to her.

She'd taken to everything perfectly, though. Her conservative, shy behavior melted away a little more each day, leaving behind a vibrant, kind-hearted woman who loved to laugh. He'd even managed to kiss her several times. They'd shared passionate, breathless kisses whose heat grew with each encounter.

Now Gavin had a surprise in store for Faith, one that should excite her beyond measure. Heading around the house to shift, intent on keeping things modest so as not to push Faith out of her comfort zone, Gavin grinned to himself.

If she had any idea how crazy she was making him, she'd blush from the roots of her gorgeous blonde hair all the way down to her newly-painted pink-tipped toes. Gavin nearly groaned as he pulled on his jeans, adjusting his raging erection. He'd been hard since Faith had fallen asleep in his lap that first night. Hell, maybe since they'd first locked lips on that dock under the gleaming night sky.

Giving himself a shake, he donned his t-shirt and

headed around the house. Faith was slipping her feet into a pair of white flats, brushing the wrinkles from her rose-red cotton dress. The dress was three-quarters-sleeve and knee-length, conservative by most standards, but Faith had admitted to feeling 'half-dressed' when she'd appeared in it earlier that morning.

"You look stunning," Gavin told her, enjoying the way her cheeks went pink.

"You stop," she hushed him, but her hazel eyes twinkled with pleasure.

"I have something to show you," Gavin told her, offering her his hand to escort her inside.

"I hope it's a salad. I've really overdone it on meals this whole week," she lamented.

Gavin scowled at her. He knew that she was very sensitive about her body, though he didn't understand why. She wasn't a featherweight, but she was stunning. All soft, perfectly molded curves, gentle slopes that his hands itched to uncover and explore. He was a big, brawny guy, and he wanted a woman who could handle his attentions. Though he'd done little more than kiss her so far, Gavin instinctively knew that Faith could take everything he had to give and more.

Still, he'd tried his best to make sure that he'd only made grocery orders that included good, lean proteins, healthy vegetables, and minimal starches. That was his preferred diet anyway, though he did occasionally cheat and eat a huge bowl of fettuccine Alfredo or an ice cream sundae. He planned to ease Faith into the concept of "cheat days" soon enough, once she realized that he wanted her to relax and enjoy herself rather than worrying about what other people thought about her eating habits.

"It's not a salad. That would be a terrible surprise," he said, shaking his head. "Come on, let me show you."

Tugging her along by the hand, Gavin brought her to the back hallway. He stopped outside the closed door of the middle bedroom, the only unoccupied room in the guest house. Gavin gave Faith a quick glance.

"Close your eyes," he said.

She pulled a face, but raised her hands and covered her eyes. Gavin opened the door and steered her inside, turning her to face the desk.

"Okay. Open them," he said.

Faith dropped her hands, one flying up to her mouth to cover her gasp. Gavin had set up his mother's old Remington typewriter on the desk, complete with a ream of fresh, crisp paper and extra ribbons. He'd added a dictionary, a thesaurus, and a copy of *The Elements of Style*.

"There's more," he said, pointing to the window seat. There he'd placed two small easels, several palettes and a dozen different paint brushes, and various kinds of acrylic and watercolor paints. A stack of blank canvases leaned on the window seat, ready for Faith's inspirations to come to life.

The final flourish was a handful of hasty sketches and scribbled notes, made on napkins and notebooks, things Gavin had found around the house in the last few days. Whether she was conscious of it, Faith seemed to need creative release, in whatever form she could get it.

"Gavin..." Faith said, her voice trembling. "This is just..."

"Don't say it's too much. You've been wearing that phrase out lately," Gavin told her.

Faith turned from the window to gaze up at him, tears gathering in her eyes, making them luminous pools of green flecked with copper. Gavin admired the proud arch of her nose, the plump fullness of her soft pink lips, the graceful curve of her shoulders as she peered up at him.

"You are ruining me," she said, the smile on her lips clashing with the tears threatening to spill down her cheeks.

"That's the idea," Gavin intoned. "I want you to want to stay with me."

A furrow graced Faith's brow.

"But why? You've done all this, and rescued me from my father... What could I possibly have to offer to you?" she asked, laying her fears out plainly.

"I'm growing very attached to you, Faith," Gavin said, choosing his words carefully. "I think you're strong, and funny, and beautiful. I'd like... I want to be with you. Court you first, if you want."

Faith's lips thinned slightly, telling Gavin he hadn't gotten the answer quite right.

"I can't just live off your charity. I'm not going to be some kind of kept woman. How is that better than living with my father?" she asked.

Gavin sucked in a breath. He knew she didn't mean to be cruel, but her words did cut him.

"I only want to help, Faith. You are free to do whatever you want, obviously," he said, feeling his posture stiffen.

Faith looked at him for a long moment before she softened, relenting.

"Of course," she said, turning to gesture to the typewriter. "I am grateful, Gavin, truly. I just don't want to rush into any big decisions, you know? We still barely know each other. How can you be sure we'll even suit one another?"

Gavin stepped close, snaking out an arm to snare her waist and pull her up against his body. He leaned down and brushed his lips over hers, savoring the burn of desire that flared between them. He kept the kiss light, short and sweet, though he wanted nothing more than to deepen it, make her sigh with want.

Instead, he broke the kiss and stepped back, giving her a reluctant smile.

"Do you want to go on an adventure later?" he asked. "There's a secret spot a couple of miles from here that I haven't shown you yet."

"You've been holding out on me, huh?" Faith asked, her voice a little breathless.

"Just waiting for the right time. I need to catch up on some work correspondence this afternoon, but maybe we can go after dinner. If you're feeling brave, that is."

Faith rewarded him with a brilliant smile.

"I think I can handle that," she said.

"Good. I'm going to leave you here, then," he said, turning her toward the window seat and the blank canvases. She gave a happy sigh, and Gavin knew he'd said the right thing this time.

9

After another amazing home-cooked meal, courtesy of Faith's incredible skills in the kitchen, Gavin took her outside and told her to change into her bear form. He went around the corner of the house, trying not to grin as he stripped and shifted. Her modesty was endearing, but he planned to strip some of it away from her tonight.

He led her north-east, away from the guest and main houses and through a lightly-wooded area. The path was a familiar one for him, the destination one he'd discovered with his brothers more than two decades earlier. The ground sloped upward in a gradual rise, growing rocky under their feet until the trees and brush diminished. The tree line ended suddenly, the trail climbing up to a rocky point in the midst of a small clearing.

Gavin paused at the top of the trail, waiting for Faith to trudge up beside him. When she halted next to him, they both looked down into the clearing. The rock smoothed out just below them, showcasing a gently-steaming pool of water. The pool had no obvious source, just a rounded lip that beckoned. It was only about chest-deep at the deepest point, just right for leaning your elbows on the edge as you soaked, and had long been a cherished secret between Gavin and his brothers. They jokingly called it their hot tub, as it remained nice and hot year-round.

Gavin felt Faith's curious gaze. He'd already planned it out in his mind, knowing that if he wanted to push things further with shy, innocent Faith, he'd need to lead the way. It would require a little courage on his part, and a lot on hers, but he felt certain that the rewards would be rich.

He walked down to where the ground leveled out and stood on his hind legs, shifting. He moved toward the pool slowly, giving Faith a full minute to understand his intent... and to ogle his bare body. He wasn't as cocky as Wyatt, but Gavin worked hard to keep his body at the best physical condition, and he knew his bare ass looked good. He just hoped Faith thought so, too.

He slid into the pool with as much grace as possible, submerging himself before turning back to face Faith. She'd moved a few paces closer, watching him with intent eyes.

"I'm going to turn around and let you shift. It's nice and deep in here, so you don't have to show me anything you don't want to," he informed her.

He watched Faith, holding his breath. After almost half a minute, her head dipped in agreement. She moved forward almost warily, making him suppress a smile as he turned and moved to the other side of the water. Giving her space, letting her take things slow.

After a torturous minute of waiting, he felt and heard her slip into the pool with a sigh.

"You can turn around," she said. When he turned, he found her giving him a tentative smile.

"Just being a gentleman," he said with a grin and a shrug.

"Mmmhm. I'll be the judge of that," she replied tartly.

"Well, as much a gentleman as I can stand. You do tempt me more than feels fair," he joked.

"Me? I'm not sure how I could be. I'm always covered head to toe!" she protested.

"Nudity isn't the only kind of enticement, Faith."

She demurred, closing her eyes and submerging herself in the water. Gavin watched her as she rose again, the hot water slicking her blonde hair back, steam rising from the bare skin of her arms and shoulders.

"I'm surprised it's so warm," she said, looking pleasingly flushed.

"It's a secret gem. I don't think my parents even know about it," Gavin said.

Faith bit her lip, seeming rooted in place.

"Faith," he said. She looked up at him, clearly uncomfortable. "You can relax. Nothing is going to happen that you don't want to happen."

"I just… I know I haven't said it, but I'm saving my virginity for my forever mate," she blurted out, her face flaming. "It would be so easy to… you know, get carried away."

She couldn't even meet his eyes as she said the words.

Gavin nodded, refusing to let his amusement show.

"What if I promise that we are definitely not going to do that tonight?" he asked.

Faith gave him a suspicious glance.

"Really?" she asked, cocking her head. Gavin couldn't help but laugh, shaking his head.

"For being named Faith, you really have little of it. I'm telling you right now that you're leaving here with your virtue intact. I would never want something you didn't give to me willingly."

She looked a little embarrassed.

"I didn't mean to insult you. It's just... I know that you have... desires," she said.

"The same ones you do, yes. I want to kiss you, and touch you. I want that very badly." Gavin enjoyed the little shiver she gave at his words. "But we can enjoy each other without doing anything too drastic."

Her gaze snapped up to his, curiosity burning bright in her eyes.

"We can?"

Gavin nodded, leaning his elbows on the side of the pool.

"There are a lot of things we can do, Faith. In fact, I think maybe you should be in charge. If you come over here and kiss me, I promise not to even move unless you let me."

Faith's eyes grew wide, her teeth worrying her bottom lip.

"You promise? You're just going to stay still?"

"Come find out," he challenged.

Faith gave him a considering look as she waded over

to him, stopping just inches away. She faltered then, looking a little flustered.

"I don't know what to do," she admitted.

"Maybe you should kiss me. You seemed to like that before," he suggested.

Faith edged closer, her arm brushing his. Gavin didn't move a muscle, his feet planted firmly on the pool's floor, his arms on the stone ledge. She reached out and placed a hand on his chest, sliding closer and closer. Her touch burned him, made him lust for her, but he refused to give in. Someone needed to show Faith that she could trust others to keep their word, and Gavin intended to be that person for her.

She looked up at him, measuring his resolve. Gavin closed his eyes, waiting. When he felt her sweet breath against his lips, he nearly groaned aloud. This experiment was as much a session of torture for him as it was a trust exercise for her.

At last her lips found his in a gentle brush. She sighed into his mouth as she pressed her lips to his, and he restrained himself enough to merely accept her touch. Faith leaned in, her arm sliding around his neck as her mouth opened, the soft tip of her tongue seeking his.

Gavin tasted her, teasing, working his lips against her in languorous movements, keeping things slow and light. She threaded her fingers into the hair at the nape of his neck, angling toward him until her breasts brushed against his chest, slick and firm under the water. His fingers flexed in place, convulsing with the need to touch her, dying to know the exact texture of her skin.

Faith dipped her free hand under the water, running

her fingers up his arm, tracing the muscles of his shoulder, his back. When her touch trailed down to explore his pec, his muscle jumped under her fingertips, making her start.

She pulled back and looked at him, comprehending his discomfort in an instant.

"Touch me, Gavin," she said, her voice husky in the steamy night air.

Still he kept himself on a tight leash, hands shaking slightly as he reached for her. He settled his hands at her waist, fingers kneading the slippery silk of her flesh. Faith leaned forward and renewed their kiss, letting it deepen. Their breathing grew heavier as their tongues danced and worked.

Gavin shaped the soft curves of her hips, her ribs, her lower back. Faith urged him on, her knees and thighs touching his. She sidled forward, only to stop with a squeak when the rigid length of Gavin's cock prodded her belly.

"Oh! You're..." She bit her lip, looking as if she might pull away.

"Hard for you? Yes," he told her. "But we're still following the same rules. You can touch me, if you want. I won't move."

Faith tilted her head, considering. Still worrying her bottom lip with her teeth, something Gavin desperately wanted to do for her, she slid her hand down his side, touching the firm muscle of his hip. Her fingers found the flat wall of his abdomen, the top of his thigh.

When she finally touched his manhood, Gavin let out a puff of breath. Faith watched him diligently, her fingertips stroking up and down the length of him. Her hand closed around him, exploring in a soft stroke, and his head dropped back, eyes closing.

"Good?" Faith asked, continuing her gentle torture.

"So good," Gavin breathed. His hands balled into fists, nails clenching into his palms as he struggled to keep himself from thrusting into her touch.

"More?"

"God, yes. Do it harder. You won't hurt me," he sighed.

She tightened her grip, the hot velvet slide of her hand already threatening to unman him.

"Do you want to show me?" she asked. Gavin raised his head to look at her, her innate sexuality warring with her complete innocence, and for a moment he was sorely tempted to show her exactly what he liked. To teach her to grip him, pump his cock just the way he liked, use her thumb to tease the sensitive spot just below the crown. Drag her out of the water and show her how to taste him, too...

"Later," he gritted out, reaching for her hand before things spiraled out of control. "I'd rather show you how I can touch you, make you feel good."

Desire flared in Faith's eyes, and Gavin reached for her.

"Come here," he told her. "Let me hold you."

He pulled her close, turning so that her back rested against the pool's edge. He kissed her deeply, sweeping his hands up from her waist to her ribs, waiting until her breathing grew heavy once more before bringing his hands up to cup the fullness of her breasts.

Faith responded instantly, giving a soft moan as she arched into his touch.

"I like that sound you make, Faith," he encouraged her. "It's so sexy. Moan for me, Faith."

He brushed his thumbs over her nipples, moving closer until his erection pressed into her belly. She gave another little moan, her eyes drifting closed, her tongue darting out to wet her lips. He brushed his lips over her neck, her collarbone, working her up to more.

Gavin took her mouth, nipping her bottom lip, enjoying the pleasured yip that escaped her. He lifted her by the waist, settling her on the pool's ledge. Before she could squirm or decry her nudity, Gavin lifted one supple breast, placing hot kisses just outside the rosy ring of her nipple.

"Oh!" she cried, her fingernails raking his shoulders.

His very male chuckle was almost more than she could stand.

Gavin took the lush pink tip in his mouth, sucking firmly. Faith's knees parted as she drew him closer to settle between her thighs. Gavin ground against her as he pleasured her, sucking and nipping and squeezing until she was undulating against his cock.

He skated a hand up the top of her thigh, his thumb trailing along the soft inside. He moved his attentions to her other breast, using his fingertips to tease her navel, her abdomen, the top of her mound.

When he brushed his fingers over her damp curls, Faith cried out. From surprise or want, he didn't know. Gavin didn't hesitate, releasing her breast and giving her a hard, demanding kiss. He penetrated her curls with a single fingertip, tracing the heat of her slit, nearly sighing at the evidence of her arousal.

"Gavin," she said, tensing.

"Just relax for me. I'm just going touch you," he promised. "Nothing more."

He slid his fingertip up to her clit, smiling when her breath hitched. He switched to use his thumb, swirling it around her clit in lazy circles.

"Just like this, that's all," he said.

"Will you kiss me?" Faith asked, more panting than words.

He plundered her mouth, tongue dancing with hers as he increased the pressure and tempo of his touch. Faith rolled her hips toward him in slow movements. He cupped her breast with his free hand, rolling her nipple between his fingertips.

"Gavin! Oh!" Faith whispered, carried away with pleasure.

"Do you want more?" he asked, working his thumb against her clit.

"No! Oh! I want—" Faith's voice rose, her pants growing loud against the night's silence. "Gavin, I—"

Her hips jerked once, twice, and Faith shuddered into his touch. She buried her face in his neck, crying out her release, her nails scoring his shoulders as she rode the wave of her orgasm.

She softened after a moment, dragging in ragged breaths. Gavin eased his hand from her, pulling her close so that he could embrace her fully. She felt so good in his arms, soft and pliant and sated. Gavin cursed his rampant, demanding erection, pressed between them and making itself more than a little obvious.

"Oh my," Faith said after a full minute, her lips moving against his neck. "I— I didn't know that happened."

Gavin actually laughed, some of the need and tension seeping from his body.

"It happens. A lot, if you're lucky," he teased.

Faith raised her head to look at him.

"Does it happen for you like that?" she asked, looking concerned.

Gavin shrugged, trying to seem casual.

"It can," was all he would admit.

Faith bit her lips, heat blazing to her cheeks before she spoke again.

"Do you— Would you—" She stopped, seeming flustered.

Gavin leaned in and kissed her, a reminder of their newfound intimacy.

"Ask me, Faith."

"Would you show me how you, um…" was as far as she got.

"Touch myself?" he probed.

"Yes," she whispered, her eyes wide. She licked her lips, shifting in her seat. The little movement made Gavin wonder if the idea of him stroking his cock made Faith horny. Her hardened nipples and skittish gaze made him think that the idea deserved consideration.

"Do you want to get back in the water?" he asked, noting the goosebumps spreading over her flesh. She nodded, slipping down off the ledge.

Gavin turned and pushed himself up to sit on the ledge, taking up the same position she'd vacated. His erection jutted proudly, and Faith turned the precise color of a ripe tomato as her gaze settled there.

Gavin reached down and circled his hand around the base of his cock, squeezing hard as he stroked himself experimentally. He spread his thighs a little, leaning back a little, giving Faith the full show.

He pumped his fist a couple of times, letting out a groan of overbuilt anticipation.

"God, that feels good," he told Faith, watching her watch him. "I'm not going to last long. You got me too hot, Faith."

"M-me?" she whimpered, her gaze riveted on the slow glide of his fist up and down his throbbing length.

"Oh yeah. The whole time I was touching you, I was thinking about what I wanted to do to you."

"Oh," Faith breathed. "Like... like what?"

Gavin cocked a brow, surprised. Faith wanted to hear a little dirty talk, did she? What a surprise she was turning out to be.

"I wanted to taste you where I touched you," he told her. "Use my tongue to make you cum. I wanted to use my fingers, too."

"Mmmm," Faith mumbled, her brow furrowing. Probably not the response she'd been seeking, but Gavin had promised her that he wouldn't consider taking her tonight. Therefore, he wasn't going to even bring it up.

He swirled the pad of his thumb around the heavy crown of his cock, sucking in a deep breath. Thought fled as he watched Faith and stroked his cock, thinking how much he wanted to take her, feel the tightness of her walls around his length as she came, trembling and pulsing, crying out. His balls drew up, his thighs and abs tensing, his body begging for release. The slow-burning lava of need burned through his veins, insistent and unstoppable.

"Ah," he gritted. "I'm going to cum. I can't hold it anymore."

"Oh," Faith said, her words half a moan.

A dam burst, fire flooding him, spreading outward from his cock. Gavin pumped his fist hard, feeling the jerk and pulse of his cock as thick jets of semen spurted from the tip.

"Ah!" he cried out, wincing with the force of it. His orgasm lasted forever, or the blink of an eye, he wasn't sure which.

When he released himself and opened his eyes, he was surprised to find Faith only inches from him. She turned up her face, seeking his kiss. If he'd thought she'd be put off by his display, he was wrong. She kissed him hard, fingers burying in his hair, body pressed against his.

He reveled in her for long moments, wishing he could have more. More than this, more of her. The more he saw, the harder and brighter his desire for her burned. But a promise was a promise, and if he wanted more of Faith, he'd have to give her more, too.

A different kind of promise, one that spoke of forever, of bonded souls.

Gavin released Faith reluctantly, pushing off the ledge and getting back into the water. Even if he wanted to say those words to Faith, they'd mean little tonight. It was easy to talk about forever after a little dose of passion, and Faith was surely smart enough to know that much.

Besides, Gavin wasn't sure if he was ready for that kind of promise. For now, this could be enough for him… he hoped.

"Let's warm up for a minute, huh?" he asked, grabbing Faith by the waist. Her eyes widened as she realized his intent, half a shriek pouring from her lips before Gavin toppled over, taking them both under the heated water.

The sounds of their laughter and splashing echoed late into the night, but not another solemn word passed between them.

10

*E*arly in the morning, Faith heard a soft electronic chirp. Once, twice. On the third time, she realized what it was and shot out of bed, searching for the brand new iPhone Genny had been kind enough to bring over a few days before.

Grabbing it, she stared at the phone number on the screen. An Illinois area code, though she didn't recognize the rest of the number. She pressed the green accept button, then put the phone to her ear, cringing. Expecting her brother, she realized.

"Hello?" she asked, her voice shaking.

"Faith?" came a woman's whispered voice.

"Shannon?" Faith asked, relief flooding her. Shannon was two years younger than Faith, a bit of a longer. She and Faith could pass for twins, if Shan's hair was a little more blonde.

"Hey. I can't talk for too long. I walked to the gas station and borrowed the attendant's phone," Shannon said.

"You walked four miles?" Faith asked, surprised.

"I got your letter from Miss Ruth," Shannon said. "I been checking the mail, now that you're... away."

"Thank the gods it was you that got the letter," Faith said. "I took a gamble."

"No kidding," Shannon mumbled. She paused, taking a deep breath. "Faith, you're in a lot of trouble. Where are you?"

"I— Don't be hurt, Shan, but I can't tell you that."

"Like I can't guess. You left with them Berans. You're still with them, aren't you?"

Faith paused, then figured it wasn't worth lying to her only ally.

"Yeah."

"They treating you okay?" Shannon asked.

"Of course. They're... It's really nice here, Shan."

"I bet." Faith couldn't miss the bitterness in her sister's tone.

"You could come up here, too," Faith said. She didn't even consider the words before they were out of her mouth, though it wasn't her place to make such an offer. If Shannon did make a run for it, though, Faith would find somewhere for them both to go.

"Yeah, right. I'm already gonna get punished for this one. How much time kneeling, you think?" Shannon asked, referring to their brother's preferred form of torment for rule-breakers. The violator would kneel on the hard wood floor, each bare knee on a pile of uncooked rice. In the first hour, you almost couldn't feel the hard grains cutting into your skin. After the third hour, it was painful beyond measure.

"Oh, Shan..."

"Are you taking that man as your mate?" Shannon cut in. It was her way, interrupting when she didn't want to talk about something. A habit that even Jared hadn't been able to break.

"I— I don't know, Shan," Faith sighed.

Shannon was silent for a long time before she spoke again.

"I hope you find a mate, Faith. I wish I could be there to see your ceremony."

"We could make arrangements, I'm sure," Faith tried to encourage Shannon. Shannon only laughed, low and hard.

"Yeah, right. You can't come home anymore than I can fly myself to the moon," Shan said. "If Jared or Daddy find out that I did this, I'll never leave the house again."

"We could still run together. We could find Aunt Ada, maybe."

"You must be crazier than I thought. If Aunt Ada has a brain in her head, she ran halfway around the globe when she was banished from the clan. I always thought Daddy probably secretly hunted her down and killed her."

"I don't think so. Mrs. Beran is helping me locate her. I have a couple of leads already."

Shannon was quiet again, then she heaved a sigh.

"Jared's going to make me take old man Anders as a mate."

"Oh, Shan..."

"At least he's not as mean as Jared. I'm kind of looking forward to it. I'll be out of the house."

Faith held her tongue, tears forming in her eyes.

"If that's what you want," Faith said.

"I'll always belong to some man," Shan mused. "I ain't sure it matters who."

"That's not true!" Faith said.

"Well, maybe for you. You think taking that man as a mate is different? You think he don't own you after you say the words?"

"I— I don't... I don't know, Shan."

"Look, I got to go. I'm not sure I can call again, Faith."

"I don't want you to get in trouble," Faith whispered, trying to keep her voice from shaking.

"Don't come home, Faith. Promise me," Shan asked.

"I promise." Faith swallowed, a single tear rolling down her cheek.

"Alright then. Be safe."

The line disconnected. Faith stared at the phone, a sob wrenching from her throat. Tears came in earnest now, and she set down the phone with a trembling hand. Those were probably the last words she'd ever speak to anyone in her family.

She jumped when the phone chirped again. Perhaps Shannon was calling her back. Maybe she'd changed her mind!

"Hello?" Faith asked. There was no answer right away. "Hello? Shan, is that you?"

"I got you," was the hissed reply. The line disconnected again, but there was no mistaking the speaker. It was Jared, there was no doubt.

Faith scrambled off the bed, barely making it to the

trash can beside her bed before she heaved up the contents of her stomach. She vomited again and again, fear filling her veins with ice. When she was finished, she sat up and wiped her mouth with a shaking hand.

She was a dead woman.

11

Faith was still dragging her feet two days later as she dressed for dinner. Genny had insisted that they come to the main house for dinner that night. Though Faith had run straight to Gavin after her brother's threat, sobbing in his arms as she confessed her fear, she hadn't let Gavin cancel their plans. She refused to be rude to Genny Beran, who had gone way above and beyond in her treatment of Faith.

Clearing her throat, Faith stared at herself in the mirror. In a small act of defiance to her brother, she'd chosen a sleeveless, above-the-knee dress in soft red silk. She put on a pair of clip-on pearl earrings, a surprisingly thoughtful gift from Gavin. White leather flats and an intricate French braid completed her look.

She stared at herself in the full-length bathroom mirror, turning this way and that. She examined the rounded curves of her full figure, not loving what she saw. At least back in Centralia, she hadn't had any mirrors to stare in. It wasn't even her shape that was bothering her, so much as guilt. Guilt for Shannon's fate. Guilt for what she'd done in the hot springs last night, for how she'd behaved with Gavin, a man who was not her mate. Guilt for leaving her family. Guilt for bringing this whole mess to the Berans' doorstep.

Gavin rapped on the frame of her bedroom, startling her. Faith whirled, blushing at being caught. Gavin gave her a long look, concern evident on his features.

"Are you sure you want to go over to the main house tonight? It wouldn't be a big deal if we just put it off a day," he told her.

"I'm sure. I need a distraction," she said, trying to give him a smile. She mostly failed, but her smile grew more genuine when Gavin reached out and took her hand. Pulling her close, he gave her a long, deep kiss.

"You are bad," she scolded, pushing herself back a step as the kiss ended.

"Often," he agreed. Offering her his arm, he led her to the car.

In a few minutes, they were standing on the porch of the Lodge. Genny swung the front door open, exclaiming with delight and rushing to hug them both.

"Faith, I know you haven't met my son Noah yet," Genny said, introducing Faith to a strikingly handsome, slightly older version of Gavin.

"Nice to meet you," Faith said, shaking the hand he offered.

"This is my mate, Charlotte," Noah told her, making the introduction. Charlotte was gorgeous, a tall, curvy blonde in a form-fitting gray dress and matching heels.

"It's a pleasure," Charlotte told her. To Faith's surprise, Noah introduced Gavin and Charlotte next.

"There's a lot of new blood in the family these days," Genny told Faith with a glowing smile. "Makes you wonder which of my sons will be next, doesn't it?"

Faith's deep blush seemed to be answer enough, for Genny spun and ushered everyone to the dinner table. They settled in, Josiah presiding at the head of the table, Genny pouring everyone wine.

The conversation was light, lots of teasing between Gavin and Noah. Their casual, comfortable banter made Faith a little wistful, thinking of the conversation she'd had with Shannon a few days earlier. Gavin really had no idea how lucky he was, having such an amazing family.

He must have sensed her thoughts, or at least her shift in mood, because Gavin silently reached over and took her hand, holding it in her lap. He didn't say anything, keeping her private matters far from the dinner table, but his touch was soothing.

"Mating ceremonies are over-the-top these days," Josiah was saying when Faith brought her attention back to the conversation.

"Oh, pooh," Genny said, waving a dismissive hand. "You're just cheap."

Josiah frowned and crossed his arms, but Noah and Gavin just laughed. Faith caught Charlotte's gaze, smiling when the other woman quirked a brow.

"Let's talk about something else," Noah said, shaking his head. "Did we tell you that we're going to Paris for our honeymoon?"

"Honeymoon," Josiah grumbled.

"Oh, Paris!" Genny exclaimed, looking thrilled. "How romantic."

"Once Max finishes his final round of chemo, we're all going together," Charlotte informed everyone.

"Max?" Faith asked.

Charlotte's smile widened, her eyes warming at the topic.

"I'm a pediatric nurse, and Max is one of my patients. Soon-to-be former patients, we hope. He doesn't have any family, so Noah and I are going to adopt him."

The look that passed between Noah and Charlotte was so sweet that it made Faith's stomach flutter. That look, that sentiment... *that* was what Faith wanted for herself.

"He's still in the hospital," Noah added. "Charlotte's cousin right now is staying with him while we're here. He's got quite a crush on her, poor man."

"Too bad she plays for the other team," Charlotte said, looking amused.

"Guess he'll figure that out on his own. I hope so, at least," Noah sighed.

"Well, I can't wait to meet him. If you decide not to take him to Paris, he should come stay with his grandparents. We'd love to have Max here. Right, Josiah?" Genny asked, giving her husband a nudge.

"Errr. Yep," Josiah answered, his brow furrowing. Faith couldn't help but giggle at the way the Alpha's mate handled him. He might be dominant out in the rest of the world, but it was obvious that she wore the pants here at home. It was also obvious that he loved her too much to nay say any of her dictates.

"That's nice of you to offer," Charlotte said.

"It's family," Genny said, as if that settled matters. And for her, it did.

"Well, I'll just be glad to get Max home and rested up. We're waiting to do the mating ceremony, until he's stronger," Noah said, ending the subject. "Enough about us, though. Faith, tell us a little about yourself."

Faith felt her cheeks heat, and she swallowed.

"Um... I'm a preschool teacher," she managed.

"Oh, that's nice! You must love kids," Charlotte said.

"I do."

Silence reigned for a moment before Gavin jumped in.

"Faith is a really good storyteller and an artist," he said. "She's got a little studio set up in the guest house now, so she can start working on a children's' book."

"Oh, is that what you needed the typewriter for?" Genny inquired. "What a great use."

"I... yes," Faith said, taking a gulp of her wine. She liked listening to everyone else talk a lot more than answering questions. There were too many she couldn't begin to answer yet. Would she write a book? Would she find a job? Would she stay in Montana? Would she and Gavin...

"Well, I'd love to help in any way that I can," Genny said. "Josiah, too, though lord knows what you'd need him for."

Everyone chuckled, though Josiah just arched a brow.

"I have my uses," the Alpha declared.

"That you do, dear," Genny said, patting his hand. "Now, would anyone like dessert?"

Everyone groaned, too full to even consider it. Soon the table was cleared, the wine finished, and everyone was getting ready to settle in for the night. Genny walked Gavin and Faith to the door.

"You should spend some time with your brother while he's here," Genny admonished Gavin. "I know you and Faith are... occupied, but Noah might not be back for a while. He and Charlotte have a lot going on."

"I will, Ma."

"Perhaps Faith and Charlotte can go have a spa day in Billings while the boys... well, do whatever you do," Genny suggested.

"Sure, Ma," Gavin said. He leaned over and hugged his mother, dropping a kiss on her head. Genny gave him a loving smile, then turned and gave Faith a hug.

"Don't be a stranger. And let me know if you need anything. I can order almost anything off Amazon, or go into the city if you need. Or you could go! I'm sure Gavin would part with his credit card for a day."

Faith gave her a thankful smile.

"You've done too much already," Faith said.

"Nonsense," Genny said. The tone she used was the same one she'd used earlier, when they were talking about Max. *It's family*, she'd said.

Faith suppressed a sigh and hugged Genny a final time, then climbed in the car with Gavin. The ride back was silent, both of them mulling over their own thoughts.

Back at the guest house, they split up and went to seek their own beds, unspoken words hanging heavy in the air.

12

It wasn't until the next morning that those words were released. Faith made breakfast, as she always did, though her stomach felt as leaden as the thoughts that weighed down her heart. They ate together in the kitchen, standing up, silence expanding between them until it was nearly unbearable. Faith couldn't finish quickly enough, washing up the dishes, planning to escape to her new office and work on her story.

Gavin watched her as she worked, brooding. When she gave him a smile and a mumbled excuse about wanting to get to work, he shook his head.

"Come sit with me for a minute," he said, taking her hand and leading her to the couch. Faith sat next to him, her eyes intent on his face, trying to guess what he might say. Was he going to ask her to make a decision right now about her future? Or worse, would he just flat-out ask her to pack up and leave? She didn't think she could bear that, not after how close they'd grown over the last few days. They were at a tipping point, but the uncertainty was making Faith feel more and more out of control.

"I need to ask you something," Gavin said at last, rousing Faith from her thoughts. She'd leaned against him without thought, her body seeking his easy comfort. She sat up a little, already mourning the loss of his wonderful warmth as she looked at him.

"Anything," she said.

"I need to know... is there anything holding us back from being together, aside from just needing time to grow into it?" he asked.

Faith cocked her head, confused.

"What do you mean?"

"I mean, is there anyone or anything else that might keep you from... being interested in taking things further. With me," he said, shifting in his seat. His words were blunt, but he still looked distinctly uncomfortable.

"Oh, Gavin. I don't know," Faith said, releasing a pent-up breath. "I just wonder... I mean, isn't there anything holding you back?"

His brow furrowed. Faith's lips twitched, thinking how his father and brother had just the same expression when they were perplexed.

"What would be holding me back?" he asked.

"I'm a nobody. I've never been anywhere, I've never seen anything. Everything I know is from books, and I'm still not that well-read. I've never even been on a real date, except here in the guest house, with you. Is that... wouldn't you want more in a mate?" she asked, finally letting out the thoughts that had swirled around her all night.

"Faith…"

"No, really. I was listening to Charlotte talk earlier. She's got a career, and she's traveled, and she's stylish—"

"Just stop," Gavin said, his words a growl. He reached out and grabbed Faith by the waist, pulling her close. "Charlotte is sophisticated, yeah. But you—"

He paused, and Faith's heart squeezed in her chest.

"I'm what? Just because I've got myself a degree from some little no-name community college, that doesn't make me anything special. I can't even take care of myself right now. You and your family are doing everything for me! It's pathetic, and I'll probably never be able to repay any of you."

"Jesus, Faith," Gavin said, reaching up to tuck a strand of hair behind her ear. "Is this why you were so put out at dinner?"

"Well, yeah. I'm just… stuck. And you, look at you! You're gorgeous, and you have a good career, and you're nice—" She paused at the grin that spread across Gavin's face. "Quit smiling. I'm just pointing out the obvious, here."

"I'm glad you find me so irresistible," Gavin said, leaning in for a kiss. He nibbled at her lower lip, making her want to sigh and lean into his embrace. With him so close, she had to scold herself just to stay upright.

"I'm serious right now. I don't think I can be enough for you. I just wonder… I think maybe I should try to find my mom, try to find my own way for a while. If I can stand on my own two feet, and you still want me, maybe then we'd have a chance."

Gavin frowned, then gave an exasperated sigh.

"Wyatt," he sighed.

"Excuse me?" she asked.

"Wyatt told you something, didn't he? Or was it Cameron?" Gavin demanded to know.

"Wyatt," Faith admitted, fresh anger growing in her chest as she thought of Wyatt's warning. "And I don't want you for your money, just so you know."

"Fucking... I will kill him," Gavin groaned. "You can't listen to anything he says. He's totally biased against women. It's not personal."

"He seemed to think I was going to stomp on your heart and take all your money, or something," Faith said. "Or that I was only interested in sex or something. It was confusing."

"I bet he had some true gems to relate," Gavin said, looking aggravated. "Listen to me. I want you, I admit that. I think you're beautiful, and very sexy. But I also enjoy you. You're interesting, and thoughtful, and you're sweet to me. Plus, you make great pancakes," he said, ending with a tease.

"All of which you could find in someone with some actual life experience," Faith pointed out.

"But I don't want someone else, I want you."

Faith looked at him for a long moment, biting her lip. Then she turned away, shaking her head.

"Hey, hey," Gavin said, cupping her face and pulling her back. "There are a lot of big questions right now, but all we have to answer is whether we want this. So I'm asking you again... Is there anything else holding you back? Not Wyatt, or my family, or money, or whatever. Anything in here?"

He tapped her chest, just over her heart. Faith tilted her head back, looking right into Gavin's eyes. He was so sincere, so caring. And she lusted for him as she never had for another, that was to be certain. But was that enough?

"There's nothing," she said finally, lifting her lips to brush his.

"You're sure, Faith? I don't want a part of you, I want everything. So be sure," Gavin said, pulling back and staring in her eyes again.

The words were out of her mouth before she even thought them, bubbling straight up from her heart and past her lips.

"I'm sure, Gavin. I want you, too," she said.

"We can go slow, just to make sure," he promised.

In response, Faith kissed him again, a little harder this time. The kiss turned heated in half a moment, passion igniting between them. Gavin cupped her jaw, one hand thrusting into her hair, holding her captive as he explored her with his tongue and teeth.

Faith's mind flashed to the night at the hot springs, to the way he'd touched her, make her burn higher and higher until she combusted. The image of him sitting on the side of the pool, stroking his thick length as he stared at her with lust-darkened eyes, lodged in her thoughts and make her flush.

"Should we take this in the bedroom?" Gavin asked. Not a suggestion, a genuine question. Even aroused, and she could tell that he was, he was the perfect gentleman.

Faith opened her mouth to answer, but the sound of

gravel crunching outside interrupted her. Gavin glanced at the door, scowling.

"I guess Noah got the same lecture from Ma about spending time together," he sighed. He stood, freezing when he heard a second vehicle pull up to the front of the house. "Two cars?"

They both stood and went to the front window. Two black SUVs were parked, doors opening to reveal several familiar faces. In particular, her brother Jared stood out, a menacing look of anticipation flashing on his face.

"Get in your room, Faith. In the bathroom. Lock the door," Gavin fired off, pulling his cell phone from his pocket.

"Let me just talk to him," Faith said, but Gavin silenced her with a glance.

"Pa, Faith's brother is here, and he brought... at least six men," Gavin said into the phone. He listened for a moment, nodded, and hung up. Turning to Faith, he grabbed her by the shoulders and pushed her toward the back hallway.

"Go! I mean it. Don't make me have to worry about you while I'm fighting," he commanded. "There's a handgun in the case under my bed. It's loaded, so be careful."

"No. No one is fighting," Faith said, wrenching away from him. "I'm going outside. You should stay here."

Her heart was in her throat, her stomach churning with fear, but she wasn't going to let Gavin put himself in danger over her situation. He'd done enough.

Gavin moved toward her, arms opening, his intent to trap her and force her to the bathroom obvious. Faith dodged him and ran for the front door, flinging it open as he caught her around the waist.

"JARED!" she shouted. "I'm right here!"

She struggled, but Gavin was too big, too strong. He pushed her behind his body, squaring off against the men who were now only a dozen paces away. Faith stared at them, gulping as she took in their simple garb and mean grimaces. Her father was absent, but these were his men, and they looked like they meant business.

"You're not getting her," Gavin growled. Faith shivered; she'd never seen this side of him, his bear so close to the surface, aggression rolling off him in waves.

"You can't just steal from me and get away with it," Jared said, stepping forward.

"You don't own her," Gavin spat.

Jared hefted a thick book bound in ancient-looking brown leather.

"Really? The Alphas' Code says that I do," Jared replied.

"You're not the Alpha," Gavin said, hands bunching into fists.

"Wrong. That weak-ass old man didn't deserve it, so I took it. I'm the Alpha now," Jared said, almost casually.

Faith's mouth went dry.

"You fought him?" Gavin asked.

"More like killed. Now I'm the Alpha, and this book, the same one your fucking father used to take my sister away, this book says that she belongs to me."

"You'll have to kill me, and my brothers, and my father," Gavin told him.

"No, actually. The Code says that if you haven't

completed the mating ceremony and the coupling, I own her. Alphas' rights. Pretty sweet, huh?" Jared said, grinning. A couple of his henchmen laughed, leering.

"Gavin..." Faith said, clawing his arm, desperate to get out from behind him.

"I challenge you for it, then," Gavin said.

Everyone went still and silent.

13

"Come again?" Jared said, strutting closer, putting his hand to ear as if he hadn't heard Gavin correctly.

"I challenge you for Alpha," Gavin repeated. Faith could feel the tremor that ran through his body, his bear bucking for control.

"That's a death match," Jared drawled, a sick smile on his lips.

"Only if you make it one," Gavin said, not backing down an inch.

"I'll wipe the floor with you. Then I'll take my sister back, give her the punishment she deserves. If she wants to be a whore, she can do it for the men in my pack. She's been such a stuck-up bitch to them, they'll love deflowering her. Isn't that right, Faith? I know you've saved yourself for my men, haven't you?"

Faith growled, pushing at Gavin. Her own bear was rising, demanding that she scratch out Jared's filthy tongue.

"Don't," Gavin told her simply. "It's done."

She stilled for a moment, and he stepped out of the front door toward Jared. Quick as a flash, she was past him and flinging herself at her brother, growling and scratching at her face.

Jared caught her easily, pushing her toward her cousin Samuel, who grabbed her by the neck. Samuel's fingers found a tender spot, making her vision go white for a moment when he gave her a cruel squeeze.

"Settle," her cousin rumbled.

"If you hurt her, you're next," Gavin said, his expression stony.

"Just keeping the peace," Samuel said, hauling Faith up and holding her fast.

Gavin stared at Samuel for a moment, then shook his head.

"Let's get this over with," he said to Jared. He started to pull up his shirt, ready to shift and fight.

"No," Jared said. "We stay human. It's in the book."

Jared tossed the book at Gavin, and it landed at his feet. Gavin gave it a sneer, shaking his head.

"No! Gavin, he's a boxer, bare-knuckle style," Faith pleaded. "He's almost killed a couple of guys. Your bear is bigger than his, you can take better that way."

"I don't care. I'll do it," Gavin answered. In the distance, Faith could hear the sound of cars approaching. Josiah and the rest of the backup, she presumed.

"And no one interrupts," Jared said loudly. "That means your father and brothers stay on the sidelines."

"And your men, too," Gavin said. "Fine. Let's do it."

Jared gave Faith a wicked look, then circled around to square off against Gavin.

"Let go of me," Faith told Samuel, pushing at him. "I need to watch."

"If you interfere, you'll be sorry," Samuel told her, releasing her with a little shove. She sidled away from him, but kept her distance from Gavin and Jared.

Jared was moving in already, fists up, shuffling closer and closer. Gavin took up the same pose, but Faith could tell that he wasn't nearly so practiced. Two cars pulled up, the Beran men and a few others running up to the circle, but they were outnumbered.

"Leave it, Pa!" Gavin shouted, sparing his father the briefest glance. "We're in the Alphas' duel now."

Josiah and Noah stilled. Jared took advantage of Gavin's momentary distraction, his left fist flashing out and cocking Gavin in the jaw. Gavin stumbled backward, but he recovered quickly.

The two circled, taking and landing jabs. Time slowed, a torment for Faith. She watched as Jared made Gavin dance, landing hard blows to his ribs and chest. She felt vomit rising in her throat, but she couldn't bring herself to move, could barely breathe.

Gavin held his own for several minutes, but Jared pushed him and pushed him, getting in three punches for every one Gavin got. Jared got Gavin off balance for a second and slammed his fist into Gavin's face, bone crunching and blood flying. Gavin was quick to repay the favor, getting Jared in the nose with his elbow, but Faith could already see that this wasn't a winnable fight.

Jared was going to kill the only man who cared about

her, the man she... yes, loved. Her chance at life and happiness. She'd escaped him, foiled him, and now Jared was going to take even this from her.

Jared tackled Gavin to the ground, landing two sickening thuds to Gavin's torso. Gavin groaned but rolled away. Faith glanced toward the house, wondering how she could stop this before it was too late.

An idea struck her, an insane idea. She tried to think, tried to come up with something else, but there was nothing. She was empty inside, a ball of fear and confusion and hatred, and there was nothing else.

She edged toward the house, glad that all the men were absorbed in the fight. Samuel gave her a hard look, but she turned her back and pretended to sob, fleeing inside. No one followed her; she was given at least that small bit of relief.

It took her only a minute to find what she sought. It was under Gavin's bed, just as he'd said. With shaking hands, she pulled the heavy black handgun from its case. She was back at the doorway in half a heartbeat, barely conscious of what she was doing.

There was only the desperation, clawing her insides, making her tremble, making her want to be sick.

Jared and Gavin were on the ground still, but Gavin was barely moving. He was blocking punches still, his movements sluggish and clumsy, while Jared grinned like a madman, blood trickling from his mouth and nose.

A glint of metal shone, something in Jared's hand. Faith's eyes widened when she saw that he had a small blade, a flash of steel arcing down toward Gavin. He stabbed Gavin right in the chest, the wet sound of it almost drowned out by Gavin's outraged bellow of pain and anger.

Then the world went silent. No, not exactly. Time froze. Then Faith's arms moved, seemingly of their own volition. Then there was a sound, a roar, and then no sound at all. Like a plug being pulled that let out all the air, but on her sense of hearing.

Jared dropped to the ground, his face contorting in pain as he clutched his shoulder. Suddenly everyone was staring at her. Faith looked down at her hands and saw the gun pointed at her brother. Only then did she realize that she'd *shot* him.

Samuel's mouth moved, and she could hear him, a little.

"You can't—" her cousin was saying as he walked toward her.

She swung toward him, gun still pointed straight out.

"I will kill you," she told him. "Get back."

Now there was no trembling, no fear. No sickness or butterflies or anything else. Just icy anger and determination.

"Get Jared away from my mate," she ordered the men.

"Fucking bitch!" Jared shrieked, his masculine swagger gone. "I will fucking kill you, I'll kill you both!"

Jared lurched to his feet, ignoring his bleeding shoulder, and ran at Faith, knife in his hand. Faith moved, and then easily, knowingly fired again. Point-blank, this time, right at the heart.

Jared's eyes went wide as he clutched his chest, a murderous look on his face.

"You... didn't... I'll... kill..." he mouthed. Or cried out, maybe; Faith couldn't hear anything. Then his eyes rolled up in his head and he collapsed in the gravel.

Samuel moved again, several of the men clustering behind him, and Faith turned back to him.

"I think I made myself clear. I said I would kill you, and I meant it," Faith shouted over her gunshot-deafness, that icy calm still in control, working her like a puppet. "I killed him. I'm the Alpha now. Get in the car, and leave, or I will kill every one of you."

Samuel's mouth moved, but he wavered. After a moment, Josiah and Noah came forward, their movements cautious. Josiah grabbed Samuel by the neck, using nearly the same hold as Samuel had on Faith, and after a moment Samuel caved.

Faith watched as Jared's men turned tail and fled. Once their cars were far enough off, she bent and laid the gun on the ground. She could hear the metal thunk of it as it came to rest on the gravel driveway.

"Okay there, Faith?" Noah was saying, stepping close and reaching for her. She half-collapsed the second he touched her, wanting to dissolve, unable to comprehend or cope. She looked at her brother's body, uncertainty flooding her.

But then she saw Gavin struggling to sit up, and all her emotions returned in a sickening flood. Angerfearsadnessfearsicknessfearlove.

Faith flung herself away from Noah, stumbling over to Gavin, dropping to her knees.

"Gavin," she breathed. He looked up at her, visibly confused.

"What happened?" he asked.

"I killed him," Faith said, her voice breaking. "H-he was going to kill you. He had a knife."

"Okay, it's okay," Gavin said, wincing as he pulled her onto his lap.

"No, Gavin, I—"

"Shhh. Let's talk about it later, okay?" he asked.

Faith looked at his blood-streaked face and felt her own crumple. Tears came at last, great shuddering sobs.

"He was going to kill you," she kept saying. "I love you, he can't kill you."

She actually screamed and fought when Josiah picked her up and pulled her from Gavin.

"Gotta get him cleaned up, girl," Josiah grunted. "Be still and I'll let you stay with him."

She quieted at that, content when she saw that Noah was helping Gavin up, supporting him and moving him inside. Josiah put her on in a chair, cautioning her to stay there.

Josiah and Noah made short work of cleaning Gavin up, getting all the blood off at least. They laid him out on the couch, trying to make him as comfortable as possible. Noah went in the bathroom and returned with bandages, antibiotics, and even a few painkillers.

"H-he needs a doctor," Faith said.

Josiah ignored her, examining the knife wound on Gavin's chest.

"It's not deep. He'll be fine. He's a Beran," Josiah proclaimed, giving Gavin a pat on the back that made him wince. "Got that quick healing. He'll be right as rain."

"I'm right here," Gavin said, his voice gone to gravel.

Noah bound the wound and made sure Gavin's nose wasn't broken, then forced the painkillers on him. That done, Noah said he'd done as much as he could.

"You want us to stay?" Noah asked Gavin, giving Faith an unsure glance.

"No." Gavin was firm. "Wait. Take the gun, though."

As if Faith had any use for that now.

Josiah gave her a long look, then sighed.

"You need anything special done with your brother's body, girl?" the Alpha asked.

Faith blinked. There was that feeling again, the numbness and ice.

"No," she answered.

"Right then," Josiah said. He made to leave, then paused, turning back to Faith. "You did good, girl."

With that pronouncement and a few more concerned glances from Noah, they were gone. Faith looked down at her hands, wondering if she should feel more horrified.

"Faith," Gavin rasped. She looked up, her stomach sinking. This was it, then. After she'd killed a man in front of him...

"Can you come lay with me, please?" Gavin asked. He pulled back the afghan that Noah had settled over him, beckoning. "I'm getting a little cold."

Faith got up and moved over to the couch, every inch of her body trembling. Gingerly and slowly, she laid down against Gavin on the couch, letting out a shaking breath when he enfolded her in the blanket and wrapped his arm around her.

"Gavin—" she started.

"Let's sleep," Gavin cut her off. He shifted and pulled

her closer, pressing their bodies together everywhere but near his knife wound. He sighed and kissed the back of her head, then settled in to sleep. It seemed like only a few moments before his body relaxed, his breathing gentle against her neck.

And Faith, for all she'd witnessed that morning, followed him sooner than she could have ever conceived.

14

"What do you think you're doing?"

Gavin winced at he sat up from lacing his tennis shoes. The bed in 'his' guest house room creaked under his weight, making him long for the comfort of his own custom-made mattress back in his Billings condo. It was one of few extravagances that he allowed himself, with his home, car, and wardrobe being simple and economical.

"Going for a run," he said, turning to Faith. She stood in the doorway, arms crossed, looking annoyed. Inwardly, he could admit that he hadn't been the best patient for the last week. Once he'd convinced Faith that he didn't blame her, hate her, or feel anything but antipathy toward her now-deceased father and brother, she'd insisted on nursing him. If that's what you called her relentless, determined pampering and coddling.

"I don't think so, buddy," she said, stepping toward him. She was wearing tight gray yoga pants under a lose t-shirt. Though her skin was covered, those pants were unfair. He could see every inch of her body, and it was killing him even more than her smothering care-taking.

"I am fit as a fiddle," he said, clearing his throat.

"You are a liar," she said, her eyes narrowing. She came closer, and Gavin's mouth went dry. In truth, he didn't even really want to go for a run. But he was trapped in the house with her, and while Faith thought he was still ailing, his libido had long since recovered. In full force.

"I'm restless," he admitted.

"I don't care what you are. You're not leaving this house until I'm satisfied with your recovery," she scowled.

Gavin's lips twitched. She was pushing his buttons, every one of them, and she didn't even know it. She was different now, after the Alphas' duel. Her sassy mouth and stubborn attitude were an interesting development, one he was already starting to like.

"Oh yeah?" he asked.

"Yeah," she shot back. She was right next to him now, staring down at him, tempting him.

"What if I prove to you that I'm completely healed?" he asked.

She huffed.

"And how are you going to do that? Jumping jacks?" she asked, a single brow arched.

"I was thinking..." He reached out and pulled her down on top of him, sprawling back on the mattress. His lips found hers in a surprised gasp, and he chuckled as he kissed her. He pressed his body up into hers, rubbing his erection against her belly and evoking a second gasp from her lips.

"Gavin!" she squeaked.

"I think this proves my readiness," he said, pushing back the thick blonde mane of her hair so that he could nibble on her neck.

"It proves nothing!" she protested.

"You're right," he said. He growled and rolled over with her, taking a more dominant position. He pressed down into her body, brushing his fingertips over her breast, satisfied when he found her hardened nipple through the soft cotton of her t-shirt.

"I.. I am," she breathed.

"I obviously have to be inside you to prove that," he teased, nipping her neck.

"Gavin, no!" she said, but her breathlessness belied her desire.

"I bet I can change your tune," he said, recapturing her lips.

"You are a terrible patient," she mumbled against his mouth.

He kissed her words away, thrusting his tongue between her lips, savoring her sweetness. She gave a soft sigh, wordlessly reminding him of her innocence. The sound tempered him, keeping his barely-contained lust at a simmer.

Faith was giving him a gift, letting him be the first, the only man who ever truly possessed her in the fullest sense of the word. Gavin resolved to bide his time, make sure she was wet and moaning, begging for him before he slaked his thirst and buried himself in her body.

"You are wearing too many clothes," Gavin said, tugging up the hem of her shirt and slipping his hands underneath to touch the smooth expanse of skin underneath.

"I'm not the only one," Faith said, heat rising in her cheeks even as she said the words. She surprised him, though by now he shouldn't feel that way. She had so many facets. Fearful girl, dutiful daughter, trembling virgin. But she was also clever and determined, unflinching in what she thought to be her duty.

Hell, she'd *killed* for him. Her own brother, no less. Should her sudden boldness be any kind of shock, after that? Gavin thought not.

So he stripped off her shirt first, baring her lacy white bra, and then rose to strip off his own. He watched her eyes widen with appreciation as they tracked down his torso, a deep flush of male satisfaction filling him.

She reached out and trailed her fingertips over his pec, down the steel wall of his stomach, only hesitating when she touched the thick vee of muscle at the top of his groin.

"You are beautiful," she told him, her hungry gaze burning him up with anticipation.

"You're stealing all my good lines," he teased, reaching out and caressing the soft curve of her hip. He slid his hand up, cupping her breast through the thin lace of her bra. She sighed again as he teased her pebbled nipple with a single fingertip, keeping his touch feather-light.

"And you are tormenting me," she informed him, shifting her hips against his. Innocent, and yet her obvious yearning was more deadly and seductive than anything a practiced courtesan could attempt.

"We've barely begun," he promised.

He moved off her, sitting and pulling her onto his lap, nudging her knees apart so that she straddled him. Giving her a measure of control, even as she sapped his. He watched her closely as he cupped her breasts, measuring their heavy weight in his hands.

She fidgeted and bit her lip, her hips nudging his. She had no idea what she did, pressing her heat against him like that. If it weren't for his jeans, he thought he could probably feel her dampness through the thin cotton of her yoga pants. Soon, she would be more than damp, she'd be soaking wet.

Gavin leaned in, brushing his lips against her nipple through the lace of her bra. Still light, teasing, stoking the flame within her.

"Gavin," she protested, half a sigh.

"Relax," he told her. "I haven't even given you anything to be greedy for yet."

She turned red at his words, but she merely bit her lip again. Waiting, trusting.

Gavin raked his teeth over her nipple, savoring her gasp for a heartbeat before he released her breast in favor of a deep, demanding kiss. The moment that she relaxed under the invading thrust of his tongue, he moved on again, burying his fingers in her hair and tugging her head back. Giving himself access to the sensitive skin at her neck, her nape. He sucked and nipped, marking her pale flesh, finding a spot behind her ear that made her cry out in surprised pleasure.

Her hands clutched his shoulders, clinging to him desperately. He slid down her bra straps one at a time, a slow and calculated movement, all the while kissing and marking the flawless column of her neck, the sleek lines of her collarbone. Kiss, suck, bite. Tease, then pleasure, then a hint of pain that fanned the flames higher and higher.

She was moving against him now, her hips rolling in a soft rhythm that couldn't be taught. It was artless but seductive, a sign of her growing hunger, one that matched his own.

Gavin tugged down the cups of her bra, freeing her breasts in slow increments. When she was bare before him she arched her back, thrusting her breasts toward his face.

"Hmmm," Gavin murmured, looking her dead in the eye as he licked his lips. "I wonder what it is that you want."

Her gaze narrowed, a pout forming on her lips.

"Is it this?" he asked, leaning in and placing a kiss between her breasts. Another, longer kiss to the sensitive underside of one heavy globe. Another just above, then to the side.

"Gavin!" she said, one hand gripping the back of his neck. As if she would pull him close, press her breast to his lips. But she hesitated, and he took pity on her.

"Maybe this?" he asked, running his lips over one petal-pink, pebbled nipple.

"Ahhh," she hissed, those hips working against him again, rubbing against his cock. "Yes, yes."

Gavin flicked his tongue over her nipple in a quick swipe, and she rewarded him with a hard thrust of her hips. She pulled at him now, arching close to his lips, her back curving as he splayed a hand over her ass to pull her closer, closer.

"Ask me to taste you, Faith," Gavin told her. He liked his women vocal, and if he would be her first, her only, he would have to show her what pleased him best. "I want to hear what you want me to do."

"Taste me," she sighed, no hesitation. No games, hardly even a blush this time.

Gavin obliged, closing his lips over her nipple, flicking and swirling his tongue over the tip. He drank in her moan, long and soft and filled with need.

When Faith's hands left his shoulders to settle on his hip bones, her thumbs brushing his waistline in burning strokes, Gavin sucked hard and moaned into her flesh. He bucked his hips up, showing her his want without reserve.

She scooted back a bit, pulling away from his hungry mouth, her fingers unbuttoning and unzipping his jeans. She bit her lip, shoving his jeans down a few inches. His cock strained against his tight boxer briefs, the tip peeking out, begging for her attention.

"Touch me," he encouraged. When she tugged down his boxer briefs and brushed the backs of her fingers over his throbbing erection, he bit his lip to suppress a strangled groan.

She found the glistening drops of precum at his tip, touching them with curious fingertips, spreading the silky liquid over the thick crown of his cock. Her tentative explorations weren't enough, they were only making him greedy.

Gavin took her hand and curled it around his cock,

closing his fingers around hers and showing her the right pressure. He moved her hand, making her pump his length several times before he released her.

"I want you," Faith whispered, her eyes flicking back and forth from his face to where she gripped his rigid length. Gavin thrust up into her touch, a groan tearing from his chest.

"Enough," he said, grabbing her hand. "I need to make you ready. I'm too big for a virgin to take without being very, very excited."

Faith bit her lip, clearly curious.

"Like what you did the other night?" she asked shyly.

"Much more than that," Gavin promised. "But first..."

15

Gavin shifted Faith off his lap, shucking his jeans and boxer briefs in one smooth motion. Faith raised a brow, but let him strip her bare too. He stepped away from the bed and went to the bathroom, returning with a shiny foil packet that he showed her. A condom, she realized.

"I don't want you to worry about anything you're not ready for," he explained as he unwrapped it and rolled it on.

His consideration of her needs filled her chest with something dangerous, something she'd felt acutely in the moments before she'd shot her brother. Something a lot like love, but Faith shoved the idea to the back of her head. Right now was about the physical, not the emotional.

Faith gave Gavin a huge smile, opening her arms to him, drawing him back to the bed. He sat down, dragging her back onto his lap again, face to face, nothing else between them now. Faith bit her lip and reached down, curiosity plain on her face as she touched him, exploring the condom's slippery surface. She took his length in her palm again, giving him an experimental stroke, satisfied when the condom stayed in place like a second skin.

Gavin grunted, hunger blooming afresh on his face.

Pulling her hand away, he grabbed her ass and brought her flush to his body, trapping his erection between them, pressing the base of it up against the wet heat of her core. When he bucked, brushing against her most sensitive flesh, she shivered.

"Oh!" Faith uttered. Gavin brought her arms up to circle his shoulders, then he kissed her. Deep, slow, and hard, invading her mouth, rubbing against her where she needed it most. He kissed her for long, lazy minutes, starting a gentle rhythm between them, nudging her body with his until she caught on, rolling her hips as her breathing quickened.

Gavin broke the kiss, spreading one hand over her lower back while the other slid between them. The calloused pad of his thumb found that spot, the one he'd teased so mercilessly at the hot springs. Delicious warmth spread out through her body, making her core and breasts and lips burn.

"Do you like that, Faith?" Gavin murmured, running his lips over her neck. Faith shuddered, barely able to nod.

"Tell me how much you like it," he said.

"A l-lot," she breathed. "I... I want more."

"Use my name, so I know you know who's giving you pleasure. Say, 'I want more, Gavin'."

"I want... I want more, Gavin," Faith said, trying to

keep her eyes open as his hips rocked, pressing his length against her, that thumb tracing slow circles. He touched her where she needed it, but she did want more.

"I love hearing you talk to me, telling me what you want," he said, scraping his whiskered chin against the suddenly sensitized skin where her neck and shoulder met, his teeth nipping her.

"I want more," she said, louder this time. "I want you in... inside."

Faith suddenly found herself wishing that she knew more, knew how to talk to him, make him excited. She lacked even the words for what she needed, but she had to try.

"I want your fingers, like last time," she finally said.

"Good, very good," Gavin praised. "But I'm going to give you more than that."

Then he was moving her, laying her out as he stretched out beside her. He found her lower lips with two fingertips, teasing the spot that ached most before sliding lower, lower.

"You're so wet for me, Faith," Gavin said, almost to himself. "And your pussy feels so good, soft and wet and hot."

Faith flushed beet red at his dirty talk, but found herself straining into his touch nonetheless. Gavin rewarded her by pressing two long, thick fingers into her core, giving her what she wanted so badly.

"Ah! Yes, yes," she moaned, her eyes fluttering closed.

"No barrier," Gavin said. He seemed surprised but pleased, slowly pumping his fingers in and out of her tight channel. "God, you're perfect. Look at me, Faith. Look at me while I touch you."

She opened her eyes, marveling at the intensity of his expression. He watched her right back, a wicked smile on his lips. He shifted a little, pressing his heavy erection against her hip, adjusting his hand. His thumb found that spot again as his fingers curled inside her, beckoning, moving against her inner wall.

"Oh-ohhh," Faith stuttered, her eyes widening. A new kind of pressure formed in her now, something that threatened to detonate inside her.

"That's right, baby," Gavin said softly, his gaze hungry. "That's your g-spot. Suddenly you're soaking wet, hot and horny. I told you I was going to get you ready, didn't I?"

Faith whined when he pulled away, pushing her flat on her back. For a moment, her heart sped up. *This is it*, she thought. *He's giving me everything I want now.*

She watched him as he knelt between her legs, teasing and kissing her breasts, dropping hot kisses on her belly that made her writhe. But then he dropped to his elbows, stroking her lower lips before spreading them wide, and she squealed in surprise.

"Gavin!" she protested. He was *looking* at her down there. Surely he didn't need to—

His lips pressed against her, making her body lock up in panic, but then the silky tip of his tongue found her— her clit, she made herself think the word— and she arched off the bed, back bowing.

"Oh!" she cried. His tongue worked at her clit, warm and hot and slippery. Her breasts throbbed, her clit ached, her mouth went dry. "Oh, Gavin, I—"

She shattered, unable to say another word. Everything was light and dark, bright or dim and hot, so hot, though she shook and shivered. When she finally peeled her eyes open, she found Gavin kissing her thighs as he glanced up at her. Normally such an intimate touch, such a ravenous expression would make her shy away, but just now she couldn't move.

"I didn't know..." she said, then she gave up and just sighed.

"That's only half of it," Gavin told her, a knowing grin lighting his face. He moved up and stretched out beside her again, his hands stroking her hip, her arm, her ribs.

"Can... can I do that to you? With my mouth, I mean," Faith asked, curious. She was so sated, her body so heavy, but at the same time, some small part of her was already hungry again.

"Not tonight. I'd come in a heartbeat and ruin everything," Gavin said with a sigh.

"Oh," Faith said, feeling a bit disappointed. Gavin chuckled.

"Believe me when I say you'll get your chance to please me with your mouth," he promised. "But you've teased me too much already. I have to have everything now."

"I haven't teased you!" Faith protested.

Gavin pulled her hand down to his groin, pressing the thick length of his manhood into her touch.

"Is that right?" he asked. "I'm hanging on by a fucking thread, Faith. If I'd stroked myself while I tasted you, I'd have come in my hand."

Faith looked at him, saw the need written on his face,

the tension in his body. He wanted more, and gods help her, she did too.

"Take me, then," she said, leaning in and kissing him as she ran her fingertips over his erection. It pulsed under her touch, making her eyes widen. Gavin ground out a sound, half amusement and half frustration.

"Are you certain?" he asked, not moving a muscle.

"I don't know. Will you be my mate?" Faith asked, tilting her head.

Gavin's mouth opened, but no words came out for a moment. She'd actually managed to make him speechless, and that made her feel a strange burst of pride.

"I could never want anyone else," he managed after a moment, cupping her chin and drawing her in for a kiss.

Faith sighed against his lips, her hands coming up to pull at his hips, tug him closer. She wanted his weight against her, she wanted him inside her body.

Gavin moved over her, parting her knees, opening her. He teased her clit again, moaning when he found her ready for him.

"You're still so wet. God, baby," he said, gripping his erection and guiding it to her entrance. The blunt head felt thicker and harder than anything she'd ever imagined as Gavin pushed into her tightness, tiny thrusts that stretched and stretched and filled her to the point of breaking.

There was a moment of pain, muscles tensing and clenching as her body tried to accommodate his length and girth.

"Ah!" she breathed, keeping the discomfort to herself.

Gavin read her, though, and reached down to rub her clit with his thumb.

Faith sighed as he stoked the flames of her desire again, easing his passage. In a heartbeat, her body accepted him. Instead of pain, there was tension, but now it was from curiosity, wanting.

"More," she said.

"Faith," Gavin warned, brushing a kiss over her lips. "We have to go slow."

"No," she said. When he didn't move, she rocked her hips against him, groaning at the feel of him, of the way her inner walls gripped him. "I want more, Gavin. Take me, take me now."

Gavin gritted his teeth, losing the edge of his careful control. He withdrew and slid home, making Faith moan.

"Yes. More, I want more," she urged him.

He thrust and pulled back, thrust and pulled back, slow as molasses. He was tormenting her. From the look of desperation on his face, Faith guessed that he was torturing himself just as much.

"Fuck me, Gavin. Please!" she begged, rolling her hips under him.

When he began to move in earnest, dragging his thickness in and out of her aching, soaking passage, Faith started to burn anew. She whimpered, her nails raking Gavin's shoulders.

"You like that? You like my cock, baby? You like how I'm fucking you?" Gavin asked, his eyes nearly black as he pounded into her body.

"More," Faith panted, her hips rising to meet his over and over. "I want... like with your fingers."

Gavin slowed and pulled out, earning a scowl.

"Don't worry," he said. "Just changing positions. You want me to hit your g-spot, don't you?"

He turned her over onto her hands and knees, nudging her legs apart and pressing a hand on her upper back, applying gentle pressure until her breasts and face were crushed into the mattress.

When he entered her this time, it was wholly different. Faith cried out at the change; he was so deep, so big, her body so tight around him.

"Jesus, Faith," Gavin told her, grabbing her hips as he worked himself in and out. "God, you feel so good."

If she'd burned before, now she was an inferno. Her fingers clutched the sheet, the muscles in her thighs shook, her eyes squeezed shut. It was intense, dark, hard...

But Gavin was doing what he promised. Touching her inner walls just so, in long, hard thrusts that made her shiver with satisfaction. He took her wholly, fully, possessing her without an ounce of hesitation.

Something deep inside her tightened and fluttered, heat spreading out and threatening to incinerate her.

"Gavin, yes!" she said. Something was happening, that peak was growing close again, closer with each punishing thrust. Gavin's fingers dug into her hips as he took her, his thighs slapping hers, the sounds of their sex filling Faith's senses.

"You're going to come for me, aren't you?" Gavin asked, breathing hard. "Do it, come for me. My mate, who loves getting fucked, who loves my cock."

Faith shuddered and locked up, her innermost

muscles clenching, walls gripping, moans pouring from somewhere deep in her chest. Her eyes rolled up in her head, and for a long moment she knew nothing but the white heat Gavin made in her body. She heaved half a sob, a thick, drowsing, dark satisfaction seeping into her bones.

"Good girl. You're going to make me come, too," Gavin said, his words harsh and desperate. He gave three brutal, wicked thrusts, a shout tearing from his throat, his cock jerking inside her body. He hissed in a breath as he finished, slowing.

Faith made a gurgled sound of protest when he withdrew, but allowed herself to be turned onto her side and pulled into Gavin's embrace. He molded her body to his, arms encircling her body, his struggle for breath matching hers.

"Thank you," Faith whispered to him.

Gavin gave a dazed laugh. She could feel him shake his head behind her, feel his chin against her nape. She could feel the way his hands trembled, too.

"What am I going to do with you?" he asked.

Faith didn't know exactly, but she couldn't wait to find out.

***

Want more? Read Cameron's Redemption Now!

Sexy, listless playboy Cameron Beran has a secret. Everyone assumes that things just come easily to him, that he's not serious about settling down or finding a mate. In truth, he's just been waiting for the right moment, the right woman. When the stars align and put Alexandra Hansard in his path, he knows that his time has come.

Independent, no-nonsense Alex is new to the world of werebears, and she's only looking for a mate to further her own political aims. When she's thrust into Cam's life, she sees an opportunity - for a business relationship, nothing more. If she happens to find Cameron wildly arousing, that'll be her little secret.

After destiny throws them together, they embark on the beginnings of a newfound relationship... a term that means very different things to both Alex and Cameron. Trust is hard to come by, especially for a playboy and his fiercely stubborn mate. When all the secrets come out, Alexandra and Cameron will have to choose, and the stakes couldn't be higher...

READ Cameron's Redemption Now!

ALSO BY KAYLA GABRIEL

Alpha Guardians

See No Evil

Hear No Evil

Speak No Evil

Bear Risen

Bear Razed

Bear Reign

Red Lodge Bears

Luke's Obsession

Noah's Revelation

Gavin's Salvation

Cameron's Redemption

Josiah's Command

Werewolf's Harem

Claimed by the Alpha - 1

Taken by the Pack - 2

Possessed by the Wolf - 3

Saved by the Alpha - 4

Forever with the Wolf - 5

Fated for the Wolf - 6

GET A FREE BOOK!

Join my mailing list to be the first to know of new releases, free books, special prices and other author giveaways.

http://freeshifterromance.com

ABOUT THE AUTHOR

Kayla Gabriel lives in the wilds of Minnesota where she swears she sees shifters in the woods beyond her yard. Her favorite things in life are mini marshmallows, coffee and when people use their blinker.

Connect with Kayla by email: kaylagabrielauthor@gmail.com and be sure to get her FREE book: freeshifterromance.com

http://kaylagabriel.com

www.ingramcontent.com/pod-product-compliance
Lightning Source LLC
LaVergne TN
LVHW011839060526
838200LV00054B/4101